D0498973

NO LONGER PROPERTY OF
SEATTLE PUBLIC LIBRARY

Bloodstone

BOOK TWO OF THE STACY JUSTICE SERIES

Bloodstone

(IT IS HIGHLY RECOMMENDED
THAT THIS SERIES BE READ IN ORDER.)

Barbra Annino

THOMAS & MERCER

The characters and events portrayed in this book are fictitious. Any similarity to real persons, living or dead, is coincidental and not intended by the author.

Text copyright © 2012 Barbra Annino
All rights reserved.
Printed in the United States of America.
No part of this book may be reproduced, or stored in a retrieval system, or transmitted in any form or by any means, electronic, mechanical, photocopying, recording, or otherwise, without express written permission of the publisher.

Published by Thomas & Mercer
P.O. Box 400818
Las Vegas, NV 89140

ISBN-13: 9781612186139
ISBN-10: 1612186130

For George

Prologue

(from the last scene of Opal Fire)

Maegan's words penetrated my head as we stared at each other. *The Seeker of Justice shall cross with one who embodies the old soil, the force of which will have great impact on Geraghtys past, present, and future. The choice she makes shall decide her fate. One path leads to unity; three become one. The other leads to destruction—which shall never be repaired.*

Was this the moment Maegan had warned me about?

"Why won't you speak?" I asked.

He looked down, his toes barely touching the carpet. I don't know why, but I plucked the sword from the drywall and lowered it to my side.

He seemed vulnerable—not threatening—standing there in the shadow of the sun.

I sighed, my patience lost. "Okay, as you can see, I've had a pretty screwed-up week. So off with the hat and glasses, and let's talk about what it is you want so you can leave my house and I can get on with my life. And if the sword isn't a big enough incentive not to try anything that might get

your arm lopped off, then take a gander at my boy, Thor."
I pointed out the window.

He peeked, then faced me again.

He looked at the carpet, contemplating his next move.
He chose the right one.

The sunglasses floated down first. Then the mustache,
then the gloves.

He lifted his head up and slowly removed his hat.

I gasped as a pool of long, red hair, the same color as
the setting sun, spilled around the shoulders of a female.

I stepped back, staring. Disbelief overwhelmed me.

Green eyes.

Red hair.

But it couldn't be. It was impossible.

I have only seen that shade of hair on one other person.

She removed her coat, exposed a cape.

And before she said a word, bells were ringing in my
ears and somehow my heart knew. Just *knew.*

*Geraghtys past, present, and future...*Maegan whispered
in my mind.

But I would have known. I would have felt it these last
few days. All these years.

"Who are you?" I demanded.

The words reached out at me, knotted around me.

"My name is Ivy. I'm your sister."

The snow was knee-deep, my leg hurt, and my sweats were
soaked, but I was hopped up on painkillers and a huge
dose of pissed off, so I didn't care.

"Stacy, wait!" Ivy said behind me, her voice desperate.

I ignored her as I marched into the Geraghty Girls' Guesthouse, slammed the door behind me, and screamed into the foyer, "Birdie! I need to talk to you right now!"

How could they keep her from me? Why would they keep her from me? A million questions swirled in my head. How old was she? Did my mother know she was pregnant when she left?

"Stacy, don't, please." Ivy spoke in a hushed tone. "Listen to me."

"This is not about you, Ivy. Just back off," I said.

"No, wait. You don't understand. They can't see me." She squealed in that high-pitched voice that only teenagers could manufacture.

I stopped and turned to her. "What do you mean, they can't see you? Are you invisible? Are you a hallucination?"

At this point, anything was possible.

"Please," she begged, "come outside."

"Tell me one good reason right now, Ivy."

"Mom's in trouble," she said quickly. "And Birdie doesn't know about me."

I wasn't sure I believed that. Birdie knew everything.

"Please," she said again.

We locked eyes and as I read her young face, I knew my life was about to change forever.

Chapter I

I made a wish more than twenty years ago and it finally came true. You know how they say be careful what you wish for? They aren't kidding.

My name is Stacy Justice, and until a short while ago, I thought I was an orphan. My father was killed when his car collided with an eighteen-wheeler on a snowy day my first year of high school. My mother couldn't handle the loss and faded away little by little until one day, she disappeared altogether.

It was rumored that she checked into a mental hospital. It was also rumored that she flew to Las Vegas to swing from a pole and (my personal favorite) ran off to Florida to read tarot cards in a trailer park.

Nothing had been confirmed.

The day my father died was the day I stopped believing in magic, both literally and figuratively. Unfortunately, my grandmother, Birdie, and her two sisters, Lolly and Fiona, took to raising me in the tradition of the Old Ways. This meant I grew up in the Victorian-era family home with crystals in every corner, herbs simmering on the stove, and black mirrors—scrying mirrors, if you want to get technical—on the walls. Birdie insisted on teaching me everything she knew, but what she didn't understand was that if I couldn't save the people I loved most in this world, I had no use for witchcraft.

You see, it was my fault Dad got behind the wheel that day. I had dreamed the night before of him falling on the ice, smacking his head into a fire hydrant. I thought he would be safer driving to work instead of his usual walking route, so I begged him to take the car.

It was the last time I ever saw him.

But I'm getting ahead of myself, because at the moment I had bigger problems than battling my grandmother.

You see, the baby sister I wished for on my sixth birthday appeared on my doorstep a few days ago, claiming that the mother we shared was missing. And as if that wasn't a loopy enough roller-coaster ride, she made me promise not to involve Birdie.

I was out of options. So I came here.

Chapter 2

Ivy was engrossed in a trashy reality show called *The Bad Girls Club*. Two young women were beating the crap out of each other for no apparent reason on the screen. On the couch, the girl claiming to be my little sister was scribbling furiously in a green notebook. That notebook had not left her side since we met.

"What is she writing?" Chance asked. A fair question, since she was occupying his sofa and her combat boots were covering his latest *Sports Illustrated*.

"She won't tell me," I said. "It's personal." Emphasis on personal.

Ivy called over her shoulder. "Chance, can I have another cupcake, please?" This would be her third. Preceded by a bag of Cool Ranch Doritos, two Cokes, and leftover pizza. It was ten thirty on Friday morning.

"Sure. Help yourself."

Ivy bounded off the beige sofa and headed for the pantry.

Chance watched her movements carefully, his blue eyes sharp, jaw set. The man looked like he had just stepped out of the latest Ford truck commercial. All-American and sexy as hell. It was no wonder I fell so hard for him in high school.

"How can you be sure she even is your sister?" he whispered.

"I can't be sure right now, but there is some family resemblance."

Green eyes, red hair of the Irish, although Ivy's facial features were more angular than mine, her skin not as pale. The build of our bodies was different too. Most of the women in my family were lean and tall. Ivy had the look of a gymnast.

"How do you know she doesn't dye her hair?" Chance asked.

"I don't, but what would you have me do? I'm in uncharted territory here, Chance. Plus, with everything that's happened lately..." My voice trailed off and I watched as a cloud passed over his face. I was sure he was thinking about my injuries at the hand of a maniac not so long ago.

"You cannot dodge Birdie forever, you know. What about Cinnamon? Have you called her?"

"Not yet."

My cousin, Cinnamon, was in Ireland with her husband Tony, on the trip I was supposed to take with Leo, the man I had recently parted ways with. Their schedule was open, since the bar they owned, the Black Opal, was currently under construction due to a fire.

Chance leaned forward in his chair and watched as Ivy sank back into the couch and grabbed the remote. My Great Dane, Thor, climbed up after her and rolled onto his spine, waiting for crumbs to fall. A train of spittle dangled from his huge black and tan muzzle.

"Why don't the, um, three of you stay here? After the guests leave over the weekend, maybe you'll have it all figured out and you can go back to the cottage."

I thought about that. Chance lived on a quiet street in a modest house with a finished basement, plus a spare bedroom. I hated to impose, but the offer was tempting. It would only be for the weekend and I had seen enough motel motif for the time being. I couldn't go home if I was to keep my promise to Ivy of not involving Birdie just yet, because my grandmother owned a bed-and-breakfast and I lived in a cottage on the property.

It sounded like the simplest solution. I had to sort out this mess with Ivy, plus I needed some answers.

Like was she really my sister?

Where had my mother been all this time?

And if we were related, did she know our family history dated back to the Druids of Kildare?

Perhaps most important—did we have the same father?

Chapter 3

I had told Birdie I was taking the train to visit an old friend from the city, so I was able to pack a few things. The bags were now in Chance's truck, since I had planned to ask him for a lift out of town.

"Ivy," I called, "we're going to stay here for the weekend. How does that sound?"

"Whoop!" Ivy yelled. "Fine by me. Chance has cable, Wii, and he knows how to shop for food." She tossed a glance my way. "Stacy doesn't even *own* a television. And the best thing she has in the fridge is Tofutti. That stuff is nasty." She made a face.

"Will you please run down and get my bags? And there's a box on the front seat. Grab that too."

Ivy ran over to us, her face open and eager. "Finally! Are you hatching a plan? Should I get my crystals?"

I turned to her. "Excuse me?"

"The box on the front seat—is the Blessed Book inside?"

"What do you know about the Blessed Book?" I asked.

The Blessed Book is a recording of our family history and theology. It's filled with stories, recipes, spells, and predictions for future generations. It began as an oral history hundreds of years ago, passed down to every daughter born to a Geraghty woman. When my great-grandmother, Maegan Geraghty, came to America, she recorded what she knew and passed it on to Birdie. Now it belonged to me.

"Mom told me." Ivy shuffled her feet a bit. "She didn't talk about it much, but once in a while I'd hear bits and pieces about the book."

"I got it." I held up a hand.

But I didn't get it. I couldn't freaking believe it, actually. Ivy was about the same age I was when my mother left me. Before then, she refused to teach me anything about magic. She and Birdie went round and round about it. And although I knew the book existed, through Birdie and the aunts, I always thought my mother had a very good reason not to discuss it with me—that she was protecting me from whatever was inside it.

Was she really protecting the *book* from *me*? Was I not a worthy enough descendant to take part in the tradition? Obviously, she trusted Ivy enough. So why her and not me?

Ivy snapped her fingers in front of my face. "Hello, earth to Stacy," she said.

"Please just get the box and your bag. And no," I said as she opened her mouth to ask another question, "it's not the Blessed Book in that box, it's my laptop. We'll do this the responsible way. No magic."

"You're the worst witch ever." Ivy stomped her foot.

She wasn't wrong, but it still stung. A part of me really wanted this kid to like me. What was the point of having a little sister if she didn't worship you?

"Just leave me the letter she left you. I want to read it again," I said.

She gave me an odd look, tossed me a slip of paper, and slammed the door. I stared at the space she had occupied, willing a sign, a vision—anything—to come to me. And then I wondered, *If she is a Geraghty, what is Ivy's gift?*

Chapter 4

You see, every female Geraghty is born with a gift—a talent she is expected to nurture until it matures enough to use for the greater good. For instance, my great-aunt Lolly was a thought-reader. If the phone rang, she knew who was on the line without looking at the caller ID. If I were to dream of apple pie for dessert, it appeared on the table that night. Unfortunately, these days Lolly was about three cards short of a full house and often forgot her own name. We plied her with liquor to avoid these episodes, since that seemed to keep her gears well oiled.

Fiona's talent was matchmaking. She could melt any man's heart and smooth over the rockiest relationship with a look and a few words. Brad Pitt would still be married to Jennifer Aniston had they consulted my Aunt Fiona.

Birdie was a healer. She could whip together a poultice or potion for just about any ailment. She was also the most powerful woman—never mind witch—I had ever met.

As far as I knew, my "gift" was communicating with the departed. It wasn't written down anywhere. Believe me, I looked. We were supposed to figure out our birthright on our own—"or we might never reach the full height of our power." Birdie's words, not mine.

I didn't have full-blown conversations with the deceased or anything. It wasn't like a ghost would pop into my kitchen and say, "Hi, I'm Tim. Can you please tell my wife the insurance papers are underneath the dresser?"

More like…messages…either through images or objects. Sometimes they came in a dream, sometimes in my head, sometimes right in front of my face in a tangible form.

Birdie told me recently that I had all the tools to grow into my talent, and by the close of my thirtieth year, I would.

I wasn't so sure about that.

Thor yawned loud and wide, popping my thought bubble. He gave me a look that said he had some business to attend to and I opened the door and called to Ivy to keep an eye on him. She grabbed her notebook and headed out. Then I unfolded the letter and set it on the kitchen table between Chance and myself.

Chapter 5

IVY GERAGHTY'S PERSONAL BOOK OF SHADOWS
by Ivy Geraghty
To be included in the Blessed Book of the Great
Geraghty Clan (hopefully)

Entry #1

My journey has finally ended and I have arrived in the mystical city of Amethyst, Illinois, from whence my people hail. (Sayonara, Skokie!) I have met my sister, Anastasia (who's pretty cool but could use a wardrobe overhaul), and am now on my first task as a witch's apprentice, tending to her familiar. I suspect I will be tested many times on my quest to rise to the height of my Power and accept my duty to grow into the Mage I am Destined to be. While my sister denies our true calling, I know deep down she is leery of the Dark Forces that lurk everywhere, and she has grown weary fighting them all by herself.

Alas, Dear Sister, your young apprentice has come! (Check that later; might sound lame-ass.)

Anastasia has arranged for us to go deep underground while we plan our mission and strategize our attack. Her sources are great (she has the coolest tricked-out sword you ever saw, a pile of magical stones, and the biggest freaking dog on the planet), and we shall call on the powers of our spirit guides to battle the Dark Forces.

Soon, we will avenge our mother. With the aid of the almighty Thor (is that not the best name for a witch's familiar?), we shall pool our forces and battle the Evil that threatens our people. Then the world will know the true strength of the Geraghty Girls. (Except Stacy's last name is Justice, but whatever.)

—Ivy Geraghty, Junior Apprentice Warrior Goddess (in training)

Chapter 6

Ivy was still outside as Chance leaned over my shoulder to read. I smoothed out the letter. It certainly looked like my mother's writing. The sweeping curls of the *Y*, the *M* falling well below the line.

But I knew from past experience that not everything is as it seems.

I breathed deeply before I began reading aloud.

> *My Dearest Ivy,*
>
> *If you have found this note, then I am gone. Don't be alarmed. I cannot explain everything here in this letter for fear that eyes not your own should discover it. Go to your special place. You will find the answers there. I have faith that you will understand what to do then. Do not go to the police and do not return to this place.*
>
> *Above all else, trust your instincts, my darling. Always, always believe in yourself and the clan of the Geraghtys.*
>
> *Be smart. Be safe. Be One.*
>
> *All My Love,*
>
> *Mother*

"That's it?" Chance asked.

"That's it," I said. "I've read this thing a hundred times trying to figure out what it means. It doesn't even sound like her." I scratched my head.

"Hmm," Chance said.

I looked up at him.

"What do you mean, 'Hmm'?"

"I think it sounds a lot like her," Chance said. "Your mom was always talking like that. Believe in yourself, you can be all you want to be—stuff like that."

"Not to me, she didn't." I stood up, challenging him with my eyes.

Chance pulled me onto his lap, scooped the hair from my neck tenderly. His voice lowered, softened. "Stacy, when your father died, a lot changed. A part of you went with him, and I think your mother too. The two of you became strangers, but I remember what she was like before that. She was kind, full of life and laughter."

"Until she walked out on me. And now she did it to Ivy." I pulled away from him. Stood. "Don't you dare sit there and tell me that you knew my mother better than I did. No one knew her. No. One."

The handle jiggled on the door and Chance said, "Okay, you win. She's back."

Ivy's cheeks were red from the cold as she hauled Thor into the house. "He peed on, like, every single shrub. His bladder must be the size of a watermelon, I swear."

Thor climbed back onto the couch, circled three times, and crash-landed on a pillow. His sigh sounded like a truck braking, and he closed his eyes.

Ivy asked, "Did you figure anything out?"

I sighed. "Take me through it one more time."

"Oh my God. Fine!" Ivy said and wagged a finger at me. "Please pay attention, this time."

Chance stifled a grin, and all I could think was that this girl had to be related to me. Only women who were related to me annoyed me this much.

"Just tell the freaking story, hotshot," I said.

She pulled out her notebook, scribbling as she spoke.

Chapter 7

IVY GERAGHTY'S PERSONAL BOOK OF SHADOWS
by Ivy Geraghty

Entry #2

Having completed my first task so successfully, my sister, Anastasia, called upon me to relay the tale of my courageous journey of perilous Danger (I mean, have you seen those losers that surf the L train?) that led me back to her and the place of our ancestors. Now I shall record my Quest for future generations of Geraghtys.

The day was bitter cold. Wind and snow slapped my face as I walked the two blocks from school to the abode I shared with my mother. Immediately upon opening the front door, I sensed Chaos. And then I saw it—the spider's web. (For those not as far along the Path as me, that means an uninvited guest. Totally handy information right there. Check it.)

Light on my feet, I crept through our small house, searching for another Sign. There was no destruction. No sign of a struggle anywhere. I continued on until—I saw it! A note.

It was brief, as if written in haste. I followed the instructions to go to my "special place." And there, between the chimney and the gutter (yeah, I like to stargaze), was a purple velvet box, emblazoned with the symbol for the astrological sign of the Libra—or so I thought. When I opened the box, there was a newspaper clipping written by a woman named Stacy Justice.

The Scales!

Balance between Good and Evil!

Lady Justice!

I must find her!

—Ivy Geraghty, Junior Apprentice Warrior Goddess (in training)

Chapter 8

"That's all that was in the box? The newspaper article and this note? Ivy, are you sure?" I fingered the article. There was nothing unusual about it. Nothing highlighted or circled, no markings. A simple story I had covered about local events.

"Well, there was also travel money. Trains are crazy expensive!" She was writing in that notebook again as she talked.

"But how did you know to come here? To Amethyst?" Chance asked.

Ivy rolled her eyes, slapped the bindings on her notebook together, and hopped on the counter. She began counting on her fingers. "Easy. Mom always talked about this beautiful place she would take me one day when the time was right. She said it was magical and that it was written in the stars that I would come here." She paused and said to Chance, "I'm sort of an astronomy buff." Then to me, "And that it was home to the most special person I would ever meet."

"So," she continued talking to us like we were her third-grade class, "not only is the symbol on the box the scales of justice, but the box is purple. Inside is an article written by a woman named Justice and the paper is called the *Amethyst Globe*." She snorted. "Didn't take a genius to connect the dots."

"And Stacy—how did you find her?" Chance asked.

"Please, that was even easier. This town is full of blabbermouths."

Good point.

She thought for a moment. "The Anastasia thing threw me off for a bit."

"That would be Birdie's doing." My given name is Stacy. It was my father's name and it irked Birdie to no end that her granddaughter was named after a male family member rather than a female.

"Plus"—she tapped the note—"it says right here. *Be smart. Be safe. Be One.*" She looked at Chance. "Be one, like sisters. I just knew you had to be my sister. You look so much like Mom."

That was when it hit me.

"Oh boy," I said.

Chance and Ivy both gave me a puzzled look.

"What?" Chance asked.

Slowly, it came back to me, the words of Maegan Geraghty as I read them once in the Blessed Book. And then—her voice inside my head. Melodious. Cautionary. Like a bird's song warning of an approaching predator.

The Seeker of Justice shall cross with one who embodies the old soil, the force of which will have great impact on Geraghtys past, present, and future. The choice she makes shall decide her fate. One path leads to unity; three become one. The other leads to destruction—which shall never be repaired.

"We have to get the book," I said.

"Yippee!" Ivy said.

Chance didn't say a word.

I hadn't understood the meaning behind that passage when I first read it, but I had a gut-wrenching feeling that it meant something now.

I only hoped I could figure it out before it was too late.

Chapter 9

The book was back at the cottage, and Ivy was trying to convince me that she couldn't meet Birdie yet. She didn't explain why, she just said she had a feeling the time wasn't right, that she didn't want to meet her grandmother until she had proven herself worthy, or some such nonsense.

"But, Stacy…" Her voice reached an octave that would shame Celine Dion. "I'm just not ready. I overheard Mom say once that she wasn't certain Birdie would…accept me." Her big eyes pouted at me as I fed Thor his lunch.

"That is not going to happen," I said, but at that moment, a bell chimed in my head. There was something familiar about her words, but…I couldn't locate the memory. Sure, Birdie and my mother had disagreements, but who didn't? And if that was the case—if she really felt that way—why did Mom just leave me with Birdie? My head was spinning around all the questions I would ask if I ever saw my mother again. *Where have you been? Why didn't you at least contact me? Or Birdie? And most importantly—who is Ivy's father?*

"Ivy, when is your birthday?" I asked abruptly.

"October fifth."

Libra. The scales. The only astrological sign on the zodiac chart that is neither creature nor human.

The date didn't help much. Those days were such a blur to me, I couldn't remember if there was snow on the ground or if the sun had been shining when my mother left. I would have to ask Birdie.

Then again, what if she was some high-strung kid who thought it might be cool to hang out with a witch? Everyone from three counties away knew my family. Plus with the business my cousin owned, the bed-and-breakfast Birdie owned—lots of tourists that came through Amethyst knew my family. This could be some kind of scam. My reporter instincts were on high alert.

I only wish my witch's instincts were too.

Ivy must have seen the doubt on my face because she backed away, cringed ever so slightly. "You...you don't believe me?"

There was a knot in my stomach, an uneasy sense that I needed to tread carefully.

"You don't seem too upset, is all," I said quietly. "If Mom were truly in danger—"

"Don't!" She held a hand to my face. "Don't call her 'Mom,' like you believe I am your sister."

"Ivy," I said and stepped forward.

Before another word left my mouth, she grabbed her backpack and bolted out the door.

Chapter 10

Show a little faith, there's magic in the night...
—Bruce Springsteen, "Thunder Road"

I plowed right into Thor and his elevated bowl of Meaty Dog in an attempt to go after her. It flipped through the air and landed on my head as a sticky hat.

The noise must have startled Chance. He charged from the bathroom, a towel draped below his waistline.

His legs were muscular, glistening with fresh water. That's all I could see from my vantage point.

Thor licked my forehead as Chance asked, "You okay?"

"Not really." I shoved the dog away and scrambled to my feet. I eyed Chance's towel, but decided on a sink rag instead.

Wiping the mess from my hair, I said in a rush, "Ivy's gone. She thinks I don't believe her."

"Well, do you?"

"I don't know, but she's fourteen years old. I need to go after her, Chance."

Chance wrinkled his forehead. "Yeah, that's not happening."

"What?"

"You take a shower, Stacy. I'll find Ivy," he said.

That sounded like a better plan.

The hot water massaged my skin as I scrubbed the muck of dog food from my hair, trying not to think about the ingredients that went into it.

I felt crappy about hurting Ivy's feelings. The truth was, it would be wonderful to have a little sister. She had really opened up to me in the short while we'd known each other. I learned that she and (our?) mother never spent a lot of time in one place, that most of the town-homes and apartments they lived in were in and around Chicago, and the last place they called home was Skokie, a sprawling suburb filled with trendy restaurants and shops just north of the city. From the time Ivy was two years old, she had been enrolled in every martial-arts class known to man. Tae kwon do, karate, jujitsu, even fencing. It was just the two of them. No siblings, no dad, not even a boyfriend. As beautiful as Mother was, that was hard to believe.

Perhaps a boyfriend would have complicated whatever she was hiding.

Or hiding from.

I turned the water off and stepped from the shower as a sudden, sharp pain stabbed my skull. I leaned against the sink, steadying myself.

The vision hit me hard and fast. A man, a knife, and dripping blood.

And then it was gone. No features I could see, no distinctive clothing, even. It was more of a silhouette except for the bloody knife. I filed it away in my mind, slipped into a robe I found hanging on the door, and hurried to the living room to retrieve the bag with my clothes in it. I grabbed a pair of black jeans, thick socks, and a purple turtleneck sweater. It was nearly March and still cold out, though not as brutal as the evening of the Black Opal fire.

I put a fresh bandage on my shoulder and thigh, grateful that the sprain in my wrist had turned out to be just a bad bruise. I was debating if I needed the sling or not as the memory of that night penetrated my thoughts. The smoke strangling me, the heat of the flames threatening to consume Cinnamon, Thor, and myself.

The pure terror of being trapped in a burning building.

It was the night of the Imbolc, a Celtic Festival of Lights known as Brighid's Day in Ireland. In Kildare, a fire is still lit every year to honor this ancient triple goddess, my grandmother's namesake. Now the pagan calendar was approaching the spring equinox, Ostara, when the earth comes back to life. One of only two days of the year where there is perfect balance between light and dark—twelve hours of sun, twelve hours of moon.

I finished dressing, massaged my arm a bit, and decided to forgo the sling. The stitches would come out tomorrow anyway. I applied some mascara and lip gloss and dried my hair. When I was finished, the clock on the stove read 12:08 and I wondered what was taking Chance so long to retrieve Ivy.

By six o'clock, I was a complete wreck. The carpet was wearing thin because I could not stop pacing around the house, checking every window, door, and my phone at least eighty-seven times. Chance had forgotten his, so I couldn't call him, and I didn't want to leave in case Ivy showed up. Thor was at my heel, eyeing me questioningly, which lent a little comfort, but I was still on the verge of a breakdown.

Where was she?

Where was he?

Sister or not, I certainly didn't want to see the kid hurt. And while there were lingering doubts—why hadn't I ever sensed her, dreamed her, envisioned her?—I vowed to keep them to myself. She needed to feel at ease until I could discern what was going on.

My cell phone rang then and I rushed to answer it.

"Stacy Justice," I said.

"Are you in town?" an annoyed voice asked. I cringed, recognizing that it belonged to Monique Fontaine.

"Uh..."

"Look, Stacy, I'm in no mood for games. There's a kid sitting at my bar right now with a bag of rocks, a pentagram T-shirt, and a smart-ass mouth. I'm willing to bet she's one of yours. Am I right?"

Dammit, Ivy. I couldn't stand Monique Fontaine. Of all the places she could have gone.

"Don't play with me," Monique warned, "or I'll hang up this phone right now and call Leo. I'm sure the Chief hasn't arrested anyone yet today, and I'll bet he's itching to."

"No, no. Don't do that! I'm on my way."

Chapter II

IVY GERAGHTY'S PERSONAL BOOK OF SHADOWS
by Ivy Geraghty
The New Book of the New Generation of the Great
Geraghty Clan

Entry #3

Curse the day I met Anastasia Justice! Curse it! Blood of my Blood, rebel sister turned BETRAYER. How could a witch as powerful as she (that's the word on the street anyway; personally, I don't see it) not feel the bond that flows between us like water down a rushing river? How does she not know when she looks at me that we were born of the same flesh (okay, so my hair is straight out of the bottle, Hot Tamale #546 or something, but still)?

Oh, the pain is great, but I shall not sway from my Quest. I shall forge on and find my mother. I shall stare Evil in the face and fight it with all my might. I shall discover my own familiar, gather my own magical tools, and the Universe will guide me to Victory!

Cautiously, I continue my lonely Journey, for the Darkness is everywhere. As a Solitary Practitioner, I shall keep my Enemies close, wherever they may be. Up ahead, I spot a refuge where I will gain sustenance, strength, and stamina. (Plus, I gotta find out what kind of asshattery goes on in a place with a neon sign of a bleached blonde winking as her boobs spill into a martini glass.)

Until we meet again—farewell Anastasia!

—Ivy Geraghty, ~~Junior Apprentice Warrior Goddess (in training)~~ Lone Warrior Goddess

Chapter 12

Amethyst was the kind of Main Street town people visited to get away from the city and step into nostalgia. Everything you'd want to capture with your camera could be covered in forty-eight hours, which meant restaurants, bars, and attractions were well within walking distance. I wrote Chance a note explaining where I would be, climbed into a coat, and pulled a hat over my head.

The nicest thing I could say about Monique is that she was charm-free. She was also a thief. She's been trying to steal Cin's husband for years. She also tried to steal Leo, Chance, even Black Opal patrons by opening a bar right across the street from Cinnamon's. Which had worked out well for her since the fire, but you could be sure it was temporary.

The streets were packed with tourists window-shopping and wandering around trying to decide what to eat for dinner. The aroma of fresh bread wafting from Giorgio's drew cravings for spaghetti smothered in basil marinara, while some were pulled toward the smoky scent of charbroiled burgers filtering from the Diamond Diner. A few businesses had outdoor speakers pointed toward the sidewalk, hoping to snag last-minute customers with acoustic jazz. In front of the small square, Buddy, the resident carriage horse, lowered his head for children to stroke his blond mane.

Down and Dirty sat on the right side of Main Street, about a block from the square, and a few doors down from Muddy Waters Coffee Shop. The antique wooden doors were painted fuchsia, and there was a sign out front advertising karaoke tonight from eight to ten. I shoved my way through, anticipating the attack on my sensibilities. Monique's bar looked like a nineteenth-century brothel, complete with gilded gold accents, velvet-papered walls, fishnet-covered leg lamps, and the woman herself.

When Monique wasn't working, she dressed to reflect the kind of man she was looking to land that week. For instance, there was a lot of leather and cheap, mirrored sunglasses involved when she went after Leo. Otherwise, as the proprietor of the sleaziest bar this side of Vegas, she usually looked like she had just stepped out of a burlesque video.

Tonight's ensemble had me perplexed.

A long blonde wig carpeted her frame, a seashell bra barely hid her plastic boobs, and glued to her torso was a green sequined mermaid costume. She was having a heck of a time scooting around.

"Finally!" she said, and grabbed my arm. She had been bent over her window display when I entered. Probably adding more condoms to the bowl. "What took you so long?" she demanded.

Normally, I wouldn't ask, but I couldn't help myself. "What's with the getup?"

She smirked at me. "Duh. It's eighties night. Didn't you read the sign?"

That didn't exactly clear things up. I raised an eyebrow.

Monique batted long, fake silver lashes at me. She wore enough makeup to repaint the Sistine Chapel.

"The movie *Splash*." She hopped backward and struck a ridiculous pose. "I'm Daryl Hannah."

"Sure you are. And I'm Cleopatra." I scanned the bar. It was early, but I spotted Madonna, Springsteen, and Cher at a table near the front of the building.

No Ivy.

"Where is she?" I asked.

"You mean the talking Bratz doll?" Monique shuffled her fins and waved me forward.

I spotted Ivy as we got a little closer, writing away in her notebook, perched on the last stool. Scully, a regular at the Opal and about as old as the nineteenth-century building itself, sat next to her, beer in hand.

From the look on his face, I'd say he'd had enough of Ivy too.

"Hey, Flipper!" Ivy said without looking up. "Hit me again."

I turned to Monique, gritted my teeth. "You didn't."

"What, you mean serve Lindsay Lohan over there? Of course not, you twit. She's drinking Cherry 7Up and that's her fifth one. But if she calls me one more name, I'll lace the next round with Drano." Monique frowned. "It wasn't so bad when she went through all the sea nymphs from Greek mythology, but then she saw me Google the names because I had no frigging idea what she was talking about.

That's when she got creative. And nasty." Monique shook her head. "Reminds me of your crazy-ass cousin."

Monique didn't ask me Ivy's true identity, because that's just the kind of person she was. If it reached beyond the circumference of her implants, she wasn't interested. For that, I was grateful.

"Thanks for calling," I said.

"Just get her out of here. And don't come back without a costume." Monique tried her best to look sexy as she pushed up her seashells and penguin-walked behind the bar.

"Ivy!" I called. "We go."

She looked up from her journal. A quick flash of relief crossed her face. Then she frowned, poked her chin in the air, and pretended to count the tin ceiling tiles.

Dammit.

Scully slid over one stool, which, frankly, was a miracle. Especially since he had carved his name into the one he had been sitting on. A memento from the Black Opal the night it burned.

Boy, that kid had a profound effect on people.

When I reached Ivy, she crossed her arms, defiant.

"You can't stay here for the rest of your life," I said.

"Why not?" she asked.

"For one thing, it's illegal."

"So."

Scully cleared his throat rather loudly.

I set my tone to firm. "There's no shower here."

Monique pumped the music up. A Twisted Sister song.

"So," Ivy said louder.

Out of desperation, I leaned in and whispered in her ear, "How will we cast a spell here?"

Ivy squealed. She gathered her things, jumped off the stool, and ran toward the door. She stopped when her hand reached the handle, pulled something from her pocket. Then she ran back and put ten bucks on the bar, said, "Thanks! Get Scully one for me," to Monique, and kissed Scully on the cheek.

The three of us stared after her, mouths agape.

Chapter 13

I sent a text to Chance, hoping he had been home by now to get his phone. He met us at the back door of the bar, his truck pristine, despite the muddy slush on the ground. He did not look happy.

Ivy hopped in the backseat, bouncing up and down, completely oblivious to the mood Chance was radiating. She chattered on about all the magic we would create. "Magick with a *K*!" she said.

I squeezed Chance's hand and said, "Sorry."

He didn't speak as he maneuvered the vehicle through crowds of people, around the corner, away from Main Street, and toward his house.

Thor hopped around in circles when we walked through the door. His tail wagged furiously and he would have taken out a lamp if Ivy hadn't caught it.

The fact that she was two feet away gave me pause. She moved like lightning.

The house had an open floor plan, so I could see most of the first floor from the foyer and felt a pang of guilt.

We had only been there a couple of hours and it already looked like a frat house.

The straight lines once vacuumed into the carpet were now blurred, cupcake wrappers lay limp on the waxed floor near the garbage can, and empty soda bottles cluttered the black pub table.

Chance hung his coat in the closet along with his keys and turned to Ivy.

"Sit," he said.

I'd never seen him so angry. Chance had miles of patience, especially when it came to my family and their eccentricities. Of course, usually I didn't traipse them through his house.

Ivy sat. So did I. So did Thor.

"Not you, Stacy."

Right. I stood next to Chance, mimicking his disappointed adult face. I had a lot of practice using this expression on other adults, but never on a child.

Thor circled around to my side and leaned against my hip. He had a bone sticking out of his mouth, cigar style.

Chance clapped his hands, took a deep breath. "Okay," he began. He paused, searching for the right words. Chance had a little brother close to Ivy's age. I guess he was trying to translate what he would normally say to him into a language females and/or witches could understand.

"I have to say, Ivy, I haven't known you all that long, so I'm not sure what to make of your actions today." He put an arm around me. "But I have known Stacy all my life, and what you did to her was…not cool."

I couldn't remember the last time I heard him use that expression. Ten years, minimum.

Ivy darted her eyes around the room and hugged her notebook close like it was a teddy bear. Or a talisman.

"You had her—and me—worried sick."

Ivy met my eyes, surprised, maybe even a little scared. I softened my face.

"You were worried?" Ivy asked me.

"Of course I was," I said.

Looking back, perhaps what I said next was not the right thing to say at the time. But I knew what it was like to be fourteen and have your whole world collapse around you. I knew the pain of feeling alone in the world. Of being abandoned. So I said it anyway. "It isn't every day I lose a sister."

I heard Chance suck in some air. My lecture would come later, I was certain. But it didn't matter because in that moment, I felt like we were sisters. And you know what? It felt pretty good.

Ivy smiled wide and threw her arms around me. I hugged her back, then turned to Chance and said, "Anything else, Dad?"

Ivy giggled.

Chance paced in front of the couch, looking more than a little frustrated.

"C'mon, Chance, I think we need to set some rules. Don't you think, Ivy?" I said.

"Like, no feet on the coffee table," Ivy volunteered.

"Very good," I said. "And no towels on the bathroom floor."

Ivy said, "No dirty dishes in the sink."

Me: "All wrappers make it inside the garbage can."

Ivy: "Take your shoes off before walking on the carpet."

"Good one," I said.

"Thanks," said Ivy.

Chance was shifting his head from one to the other of us. Finally he broke into a smile.

"Did we miss anything?" I asked him.

He looked straight at me. "No running away."

Ivy fielded the statement by saying, "I promise."

But I knew what he meant. Chance had taken it personally when I didn't come back after college. He had been there for me through everything. He knew my family like he knew his own, and he never believed that I just wanted to see the world, wanted more out of life than one could ever find in a single-stoplight town.

Now that I was back, it was hard to convince him otherwise. Because the truth was, I had loved him; even when I said good-bye, I had loved him.

But that was a long time ago.

"Me too," I said.

His eyes darkened and a sultry look crossed his face. For a moment, I thought he would kiss me. Instead he said, "And"—he pointed to Thor—"no sleeping on the furniture."

Thor's huge jaws parted and he let out a high-pitched whine.

"No," Chance said.

My dog rolled on his back, the tan coat nearly melting into the beige carpet, and kicked his legs in the air. Ivy bent down to give him a belly rub.

"I'm starving," she said.

Chance said, "Ivy, why don't you get settled in the downstairs bedroom and we'll order some food? Do you like Chinese?"

"Is chop suey Chinese?" she asked.

"Yes."

"Then yes." She popped off the couch and said, "C'mon, Thor."

Thor looked to me for approval, and I gave him a hand signal, indicating he could follow. Ivy strapped her backpack to him and the pair lumbered down the basement stairs.

"How about a glass of wine?" Chance asked.

"Sounds good."

Chance opened a drawer and pulled out a menu, then reached for a bottle of Shiraz. "You think that was a good idea, calling her your sister?"

I shrugged as I sipped my wine. "What harm could it do?"

If I had seen the penny before then, I might have known.

Chapter 14

IVY GERAGHTY'S PERSONAL BOOK OF SHADOWS
by Ivy Geraghty

Entry #4

I have passed another test in my schooling as a young witch's apprentice. I have proven faithful, loyal, and, above all, steadfast in my quest to become a powerful jewel in the Crown of the Great Geraghty Clan. (Okay, so I took a little detour, but I made an ally, so it was like, totally written in the stars. Shout-out to Scully!)

Phase II of my progress has begun as my sister, Anastasia Justice, has finally embraced me as one of her own. She has promised to perform a Spell and her familiar, the almighty Thor, has been granted permission to allow me to practice my skills of training a familiar to guard his Priestess. (I could do without his anal acoustics, but no pain, right?)

More importantly, I have identified an Enemy within our midst. Immediately upon entering her sanctuary, I knew that the woman who calls herself Monique (seriously, does anybody think those frontal lobes are real?)

is an anti-pagan. My people have struggled for years, nay, centuries to snuff out such hatred, and I, as the newest member of the Geraghty Clan, shall single-handedly turn her head, if not her heart, to the Light! (Okay, so all she did was call me Sabrina, but she's not the sharpest knife in the drawer, so it should be a cakewalk.)

—Ivy Geraghty, Junior Apprentice Warrior Goddess (in training)

Chapter 15

As we waited for the food to arrive, I discussed with Ivy
the very real possibility that in a situation like this, Birdie
might be the only one that could help. She didn't like the
idea, but acquiesced to the plan of heading to the cottage
to get the book, and if there was nothing in there—nothing
in Maegan's predictions about a missing Geraghty—then
we would go to Birdie and the aunts. Of course, I had to
promise that we would work a spell and that I would gather
all the magical tools I had in my possession. This amounted
to a few crystals, a sword, and a charm hanging in my doorway. All gifts from the Geraghty Girls. I didn't even have
a cape. For some reason, I could never keep them clean.

"You don't remember anything from your teachings?
There was nothing in the pages of the book about our
mother being in danger?" she asked.

Chance excused himself when the doorbell rang. I
called him a coward under my breath. Boy, was I going to
be a disappointment to this kid.

"Ivy, the truth is, I'm about as new at this as you are.
I learned a lot when I was kid, younger than you even,

but something...happened...and I stopped...practicing."
I wasn't ready yet to discuss my father. Wasn't ready to
know if she remembered any mention of him, or if my
mother had tossed his memory aside like she did me.
"The first time I even laid eyes on the book was a few
weeks ago."

I didn't say that it was the first time I even wanted to
see it, or the first time anyone had trusted me with it. The
night Birdie gave it to me, I pored over everything I could,
mostly to keep her off my back because I was sure she
would have quizzed me sooner or later, but also because
it fascinated me. The stories, the lore, the recipes. It was
as if I were in the center of a women's circle, soaking up
their wisdom, their light, their magic.

Still, the thing was thicker than *War and Peace*. It would
take a lifetime to read all of it. I wondered if by then, I
might start to actually feel like a witch.

Geez, I hoped not.

Ivy looked surprised. "But I've heard things about your
talent when I was looking for you. People around here think
you're a pretty powerful witch."

The thought of Ivy wandering around town talking
to strangers made me shudder. Amethyst had more Froot
Loops than a box of Kellogg's. I was pretty sure the town
mascot was officially a Whackadoodle.

"Sweetie, people around here also think that the Cubs
will win the World Series and that Old Style is the elixir of
the gods. Don't believe everything you hear."

Or see, for that matter.

"And don't talk to strangers," I added. Seemed like the
situation called for it.

Chance came into the kitchen with two brown paper bags. He set them on the counter while I hunted for plates and napkins.

Behind me, Ivy said, "I got this."

She tossed two twenty-dollar bills on the table and ripped open the first bag.

Chance and I exchanged a look.

I said, "Ivy, where is all this money coming from?"

She shrugged, pulled a bulging white carton from the bag. Steam poured from the lid as lo mein noodles spilled over the sides.

"I told you. Mom left me some money."

How much money did she leave her? I set the plates on the counter and went for some silverware. It was none of my business, but now that she was in my care, I wondered if perhaps it was dangerous for a teenager to have too much cash on her. Then again, that might have been the last of it.

"Put your money away, Ivy," Chance said.

"It's okay. I want to chip in," she said.

The ten bucks she had laid on the bar earlier was in my pocket. I had flipped Monique my own money and tried to return Ivy's to her, but she had argued with me the entire time it took for Chance to arrive to pick us up, so I let it go. I figured I would sneak it into her backpack when she wasn't looking.

Sometimes you have to pick your battles. I shook my head at Chance and he let the money sit there.

The second bag was screaming my name. I reached for the beef with broccoli and set it on a plate. We gathered around the pub table, the three of us exchanging sauces and food. We made small talk as we ate, and Ivy offered me an egg roll.

It was perfectly crunchy with just a hint of oil. I dabbed a napkin around it and bit in, listening to Ivy and Chance talk about the Wii match they would have over the weekend. Billiards, tennis, Mario, and a game called Black Ops, which I was about to protest until I bit into something metallic.

I grabbed a napkin and spit into it.

Ivy made a face. "Ew, that's vile, Stacy."

"Tell me about it," Chance said. Then he looked at my face. "You okay?"

"That didn't taste right." I opened the napkin, examining the contents.

There, between the cabbage and the carrots, was a penny.

I dumped the egg roll onto my plate and walked to the garbage. My thumb on the penny, I slid the contents of the plate into the trash and headed for the sink.

When I didn't make a fuss about tasting the head of our sixteenth president, Ivy knew something was up.

Chance folded himself into the refrigerator, carefully lining up the leftover cartons and avoiding eye contact while I offered to take the garbage out.

"What's with the weirdness all of a sudden?" Ivy asked.

No one answered her.

"Fine! Don't tell me, but you know I'll find out sooner or later." She stomped into the living room and turned on the television.

Later, please. Much later.

Outside, I took the penny from where I had stashed it and looked at the date.

Just as I had feared.

The year Ivy was born. Or at least the year she says she was born. Or the year she was told she was born.

Birdie taught me from an early age that pennies were sent from our spirit guides. According to her, those who passed on left us little messages in the shape of a molded piece of copper. Not just me, but everyone. Mostly, the message simply said, "Hi, I'm doing fine. Thinking of you."

But not always.

The day she told me that, my father had been dead for three months. We were gardening—planting rosemary in remembrance of him. I stuck a steel trowel in the mud and, along with a clump of soil, out popped a penny.

It was a bright shiny copper, the color of Birdie's hair, not dull as you might expect a penny buried in the dirt to be.

She looked at the date and noted that it was the year my father had come into this world.

"There, now," she said. "You see that, Anastasia? That is your father waving hello."

There are rules to reading these messages. A penny cannot just be lying in the street. You can't walk into a grocery store, see a penny on the floor near the cucumbers, and assume it was sent from a spirit guide. It has to be in an unusual place. Like on top of a lamp. Or in an egg roll.

Here's what Birdie hadn't known then. And still didn't today.

Weeks before my father's crash, I was finding pennies stamped with the year he was born *everywhere*. In my sock drawer. In my locker at school. Inside my gym shoes. Once,

I even found one at the bottom of an ice-cream cone. Coincidence? I think not.

So to me they are more than a wave. They are a warning.

Right now, all I could think about was the danger waiting for me—for us—just around the corner.

Chapter 16

IVY GERAGHTY'S PERSONAL BOOK OF SHADOWS
by Ivy Geraghty

Entry #5

Tonight marks the start of our Mission. Anastasia and I will stealthily break into her cottage and retrieve the Blessed Book (right, so she has a key, but we're still going incognito so as not to disturb the Old One). It is the treasure that holds the secret to the whereabouts of our mother. I am certain of it!

We shall tread quiet as mice. Slink careful as cats. And then, finally, we will have the Knowledge that will lead us to our mother's Salvation. We shall slay those who have taken her (or at least kick 'em in the nads), and Victory shall be ours!

P.S.: There's something freakalicious about the whole penny-in-the-egg-roll thing. Can't wait to crack that code.

—Ivy Geraghty, Junior Apprentice Warrior Goddess (in training)

Chapter 17

A few hours later, dressed head to toe in all black (Ivy's idea), we left Chance's house and headed up the hill to the inn. Thor wanted to come with us, but since the Geraghty Girls thought Chance was doggie sitting, I decided it might not be a good idea to have Thor wandering around the property, coating the windows with slobber. To Thor, giant house equaled warm, yummy food. Fiona spoiled the crap out of him, fixing him pot roast and mashed potatoes every Sunday. Which more than made up for the fact that Lolly treated him like a dress-up doll.

The streets were bare, lit only by a few scattered streetlights and a sliver of moon. Aside from a few raccoons robbing a garbage can, the town was deadly quiet.

The porch light glowed at the house, highlighting her best features. The Queen Anne was well over a century old, dripping with gingerbread, its ornate spindles and turrets painted in complementary shades of teal, red, and purple. It was the details that made it stand out from the rest of the homes on the block. Amethyst boasted many architectural gems in various styles, from Italian Renaissance to Federal brick, but something about the Geraghty Girls' Guesthouse beckoned you to step inside and discover her secrets.

My maternal great-grandfather, who willed the house to his three daughters when he passed away, built it. Since none of them had a husband at that stage in their lives, they decided to turn it into a bed-and-breakfast.

There were three cars in the driveway. Presumably the three guest rooms were full. There was no movement from inside and just a few lights were on. Wine-and-cheese hour had long passed, so most likely everyone was either asleep or enjoying a nightcap on Main Street.

The black wrought-iron gate framed only the main house, so I tapped Ivy and pointed toward the cottage, and she nodded.

We hurried along the side of the property and headed straight for the back door of the cottage. I shoved the key into the lock but didn't need to twist it.

The door creaked open.

I hesitated, looking for a spider's web or some sign that someone had been there. Birdie had taught me long ago—and I had since learned it was laser-beam accurate—that a spider's web netting a doorway meant an uninvited guest had come into your home.

Ivy whispered, "Did you forget to lock it?"

I put my finger to my mouth and shook my head. After years of living in the city of Chicago, I would never leave a door unlocked.

She cupped a hand over my ear and whispered again. "What should we do?"

I stood perfectly still, listening to my body, trying to decide if I had nausea or just a gut feeling that something wasn't right.

Nothing.

Quietly as I could, I told Ivy to wait on the stoop and entered the cottage.

The back door emptied into the kitchen, which spilled into the living room. There was one bedroom to the left and a bathroom to the right. I didn't have a flashlight and I was afraid to turn on any other lights because I didn't want to alert Birdie or the aunts to my presence.

What to do?

I decided that if there were someone in the cottage, the Geraghty Girls would be the least of my problems.

Just before my hand hit the switch, Ivy whispered loudly, "Stacy."

I turned and she tossed me a penlight.

The kid reminded me of Inspector Gadget.

I gave her a thumbs-up and turned it on, pointing it around the cottage from where I stood in the kitchen.

"Son of a pussbucket," I said softly.

"What? What is it?" Ivy asked.

"Fiona redecorated." I didn't bother to hide my irritation.

When I first moved into the cottage it looked like the inside of a genie bottle. Slowly, I had given the place a more scaled-down decor thanks to the clearance sales at Pier 1 Imports.

Now, it looked like a club on the corner of a red-light district. Red and pink velvet everywhere, a leopard-print sofa shaped like lips, and more beads than a topless drunk girl at a Mardi Gras parade.

What the hell did she do that for? It would take weeks to get the scent of jasmine out of the carpet.

"Is it okay to come in?" Ivy asked.

Fiona had probably just forgotten to lock the back door.

"It seems to be. Come on. The book should be in my bedroom," I said.

We crept quietly and I wondered where Moonlight could be. He was my little white cat I had brought with me when I moved back to Amethyst. Fiona had said she would care for him while I was "out of town," but I doubted that meant he could stay at the inn. Maybe he was on the prowl.

Ivy was right behind me as we made our way toward the bedroom door. I couldn't help but notice that my desk, my chair—even the sword Birdie had given me—was gone.

"Where is all my stuff?" I muttered.

The handle on the bedroom door squeaked then. And rotated.

That's the problem with my "gift." The dead never show up when you need them.

Chapter 18

Ivy clutched my coat behind me, and I said, "Go!"

She turned and catapulted forward so fast she was airborne. I followed, but being the sister with all the grace of a newborn giraffe, I tripped over the stupid sofa and landed face-first in the carpet. My consolation prize was a rug burn across my chin.

The door flew open hard enough to bang against the wall. I was sure there would be a dent from the impact. "Who the hell are you?" A man's voice. Deep. Angry. Like a volcano that had swallowed one too many virgins and had a serious case of indigestion.

I was on all fours, ass poking in the air. Not exactly a good first impression. Especially since my legs were my best feature.

I lifted my head and noted that Ivy, thankfully, was nowhere in sight.

"John? Honey?" A woman's voice.

Crap.

I could pretty much piece together what was going on at that point. I started to get up and heard a soft click.

Then again, I'd been wrong before. I flattened my body back into the carpet, wishing to the gods I had brought Thor.

"Go back to bed, Deirdre," John said, and when I heard the door shut I figured Deirdre knew better than to argue with him.

"I'll ask you again, real slow so we understand each other. What the hell are you doing here?" Chicago accent. Probably a Sox fan. I hated Sox fans. There's a reason they call that park the Cell. Actually it's Cellular Field, but double entendre and all that.

Any light from the moon had scurried away to the corners of the cottage. There was only blackness.

I found a voice, but it wasn't mine. It was on loan from a Muppet. "I, I, actually used to live here."

"You always break into houses you used to live in?"

Youdsed. He actually said *youdsed.* I had a sudden urge to empty my bladder. And to order an Italian sausage sandwich.

"What I mean is, I live here." Until my aunt sold me out. Dammit, Fiona. "You rented this place, right? For a week, probably? The Geraghtys are my family."

My voice sounded more like my own by then, and John told me to stay put.

"Why you sneaking around in the dark?" he asked.

Good question. I thought fast. "Um, well, I needed something...from my bedroom." I flung an arm behind me. "And, I, well, I, um, gee—"

"What are you, retarded?"

Whoa, that was uncalled for! How do these people choose my family to spend their vacation with? "Hey, that

is an offensive word! People with mental disabilities prefer
to be called 'challenged.' I think. Anyway, it's something
like that, but if you must know, no, I'm not. Challenged,
that is."

"Turn around, sweetheart."

I hated to be called sweetheart more than I hated Sox
fans. I was still doing the breaststroke in the carpet fac-
ing away from him, so I wasn't quite sure what he meant
by "turn around." I considered rolling over like a dog for
a moment but opted instead for an all-fours three-point
turn.

"Stand up."

I did.

"Turn on the light."

I did. Wish I hadn't.

As soon as my eyes adjusted to the light, I caught a full-
on shot of John buck-ass naked. The pistol he was sporting
was larger than any I had ever seen.

So was the gun.

I shut my eyes.

"Deirdre?" I called.

John chuckled. Apparently my squeamishness was
amusing him.

Deirdre poked her head out the door as I opened one
eye.

She must have realized there was some kind of mistake.
"John, put your pants on!" She opened the door wider to
allow him inside.

We looked at each other for a minute. She had all
the curves of a champagne flute with a shock of jet-black
hair. The doily on the coffee table was less revealing than

Deirdre's negligee. I could see some sort of tattoo wrapped around her thigh.

"You must be on your honeymoon." I was mortified.

Deirdre cocked her head and nodded.

"I'm so sorry. I'll be out of here in a minute. I was just looking for a book."

Ivy said, "Stacy! That's a secret."

Deirdre raised an eyebrow. "Come out from there," she called.

Ivy scooted into the doorframe and Deirdre's face relaxed. She smiled at Ivy, her eyes so blue I could see waves crashing through them. The woman appeared to be in her mid-thirties.

Deirdre looked at me. "I got a sister too. The things they put you through, huh?" Deirdre said. "C'mon, sit, I'll make coffee."

On my reverse bucket list of the top ten things I never wanted to experience, sharing a honeymoon with the Sopranos and Buffy the Vampire Slayer would rank right up there.

"No," I said hurriedly. "We should get going. I cannot tell you how sorry I am to interrupt your honeymoon." I pushed Ivy toward the back door.

John came out of the room with his pants buckled and his shirt unbuttoned.

"Whoa," Ivy said.

"Don't stare." I tapped her shoulder.

"Did you see the size of that gun?" she asked.

I hoped she was talking about the Glock in his holster.

"You girls need a ride somewhere?" John asked.

Before I could clamp my hand over Ivy's mouth, a sickening scream pierced the walls.

Chapter 19

A fear of weapons is a sign of retarded sexual and emotional maturity.
—Sigmund Freud

Ivy jumped and Deirdre yelped. John rushed to the window, hand on his holster.

"What was that?" Deirdre demanded.

I hugged Ivy close to me, wondering the same thing. It wasn't a playful scream. It was a scream of pure terror. And it came from the direction of the Geraghty Girls' Guesthouse.

John parted the thick curtains, tassels smacking his face. "Get dressed, Deirdre."

"Do you see anything?" she asked.

He shook his head. "Just get dressed." Deirdre rushed into the bedroom, and I began inching closer to the door, tucking Ivy behind my back.

John tossed a look over his shoulder. "You two stay put."

My body began prickling, a twitchy, nervous feeling that told me something was not right. There was no nausea, which is what usually hit me when I encountered a man holding a gun, but something bad was about to happen.

Every inch of me felt it.

I said, "I think it's best if we left."

"I didn't ask what you think." John started buttoning his shirt.

Gun or not, this machismo act was pissing me off.

"Look, unless you plan to tie us up and hold us hostage, we're leaving." I turned to the door.

Ivy looked at me like I had lost my mind.

"Wait a second," John said. "Wait one freaking second there."

I turned back, praying to the Goddess Morrigan he didn't have the gun pointed at me. "Don't I know you?" he asked.

"Nice try," I said.

"No, I do." He snapped his fingers. "You're Stacy, ain't you?"

Ivy widened her eyes.

I tensed. This man did not look familiar. "How do you know my name?"

John laughed. "Holy crap! Hey, Deirdre, get out here!"

What the heck was happening here? "Who are you?"

Deirdre came out of the bedroom wearing a tight-knit turquoise dress, hair teased to the ceiling.

"This is Stacy," John said to her.

Deirdre clapped her hands, and I was growing ever more uncomfortable.

"Well, you are a doll!" Deirdre said.

John said, "Hey, ain't you supposed to be on vacation?"

How could he know that? I didn't like how this scenario was playing out one bit.

I could hear muffled voices outside then, and John peeked out the window. "Uh-oh," he said and looked at Deirdre, then me. "We got trouble."

"Seriously, who the hell are you people?" I said, not bothering to hide my frustration. I felt like I was trapped in a Dashiell Hammett film, except without the witty banter.

Deirdre rushed to the window, peered over John's shoulder, and said, "I'll call Leo."

"Get my badge too, honey," John told her.

Leo? Badge? "You're a cop?" I asked.

John gave me a wicked grin. "I think the term is peace officer." He enunciated the words perfectly.

Chapter 20

IVY GERAGHTY'S PERSONAL BOOK OF SHADOWS
by Ivy Geraghty

Entry #6

Alas, the Great Book remains just out of our grasp! It seems that my sister's home has been intruded upon, and just when we were about to battle the trespassers, a scream cut through the walls!

Rushed into the dark night, we have been forced to face an unforeseen obstacle (actually they kicked me back to the porch). I have full confidence that Anastasia will settle the matter with me as her most faithful servant and our Mission shall continue. My meeting with Brighid must wait another day. I am off to my secret Lair.

—Ivy Geraghty, Junior Apprentice Warrior Goddess (in training)

Chapter 21

A visibly shaken elderly woman stood on the front lawn of my grandmother's bed-and-breakfast in her pajamas. Next to her, I assumed, was her husband, who could have passed for Father Time.

Deirdre was on the phone with Leo, and John was trying to extract what had happened from the woman, while the old man stood next to her, shivering and looking annoyed.

The screams from the woman's throat grew louder, and I was sorry that whatever had upset her hadn't happened after she washed off her makeup. She looked like a Picasso left in the rain.

The woman was pointing toward the house. I had no idea what had transpired, but from personal experience, I thought it best not to subject Ivy to it. I asked her to wait on the porch.

Just as John called me over I heard Ivy say, "No worries. I'll just go text Scully."

I swiveled around. "What? No, don't do that."

She dashed off.

"Stacy, come over here, would ya?" John said. In the light from the porch, I could see he was a generation older than his bride. "Can you please translate for me? I don't speak Blubberish."

Man, this guy got under my skin. "What makes you think I do?"

"Ask her what happened." John flipped out a notebook. "The husband says he didn't see nothing, the wife went to use the john and came out all cuckoo for Cocoa Puffs."

Deirdre was still on the phone and gave me an encouraging smile.

The house had a lot more lights on, but there was no sign of Birdie or the aunts.

That feeling came again. An itchy, twitchy sensation.

The woman looked at me, although I wasn't sure what she could see through the sea of mascara muddying her eyeballs.

Her face looked a little more horrified when she took in my attire.

"Are...y-y-y-yooou with, with, the p-p-p-p-p-olice?" she asked between sobs.

"Sure, why not." Then I smiled at her. In a soft voice, I asked, "Can you please tell us what happened?"

She nodded and took in a series of long breaths that looked a lot like hyperventilation protocol.

Quickly, I asked her husband, "What's her name?"

"Cece Honeycut."

Her hands were trembling as I reached for them. "Mrs. Honeycut, please tell us what you saw. Why are you so upset?"

"It was...just...so, so...awful."

Her hands grew warm, despite the chilly night, then fiercely hot between mine, and a pain shot through my skull.

"Leo's on his way," Deirdre said to my right.

It came in a flash, so quick I nearly missed it.

Deirdre asked, "Did someone get hurt or hurt you, Mrs. Honeycut?"

Mrs. Honeycut looked at her husband just as the vision faded from my mind.

At the same time, we both said, "Blood."

Chapter 22

Deirdre got back on the phone with Leo, who probably just assumed the woman was hysterical because of something my grandmother had done. He himself had been known to lose his marbles in the presence of Birdie.

I dropped Mrs. Honeycut's hands and flew to the front door of the bed-and-breakfast. Locked. "Mrs. Honeycut, I need the key!"

She shook her head and her husband said, "We left it."

The vision was of a double-edged blade that flashed red. I wasn't an expert at reading these things, but I could guess that red meant blood and blood was bad. The problem, I feared, was that if someone had broken into the house to cause harm, Birdie and the aunts would hear nothing back in the private quarters. The walls were thick and reinforced with extra insulation so guests wouldn't disturb them and vice versa.

I leaned on the bell that rang only in the back part of the house. The old-fashioned crank bell chimed in the front. "Birdie, Fiona, Lolly! Open the door!"

John was behind me then and I heard a siren approaching.

After a minute, I saw a silhouette through the glass.

The door opened and there stood my aunt Lolly, her hair molded into a pageboy. She wore a pink ball gown with more taffeta and tulle than a bridal shop and a rhinestone necklace that looked to be choking her.

Lolly always dressed as if the queen of England might pop over any moment.

"Hello," she said. "I'm sorry, but we're all booked up." Not a spark of familiarity.

John started to say something, but I put a finger up and gave him a look I hoped he understood.

Lolly's lipstick hadn't quite made it between the lines, and her eyebrows had been shaved off, then drawn in with what must have been a Sharpie. That coupled with the fact that she didn't recognize me told me the key was in the ignition but the car was out of gas.

"Aunt Lolly, it's me, Stacy. Is Fiona home? Or Birdie?"

"One moment, please." Lolly slammed the door just as Leo pulled into the parking lot.

Not a minute later, Fiona opened the door wearing a gold peignoir set. It was after nine, so she was probably getting ready to call it a night, but I still couldn't believe she would dress like that with guests in the house.

She smiled warmly at John, batted her lashes, then said, "Stacy, you're back," in a voice that purred. Fiona made Ann-Margret look like a transgender meter maid. "Don't they have makeup where you were visiting, dear? And why are you dressed like a cat burglar?" To John she said, "She's such a pretty girl, I don't know what we'll do with her."

She opened the door wide, inviting us inside, and I heard John explaining the Cece situation as I went to search for my grandmother.

The house had thirteen rooms. The entryway led to a parlor where guests were greeted with a warm fire and hot snacks. To the left of that was a staircase that trailed to the three upstairs guest rooms. The dining room was at the end of the hall on the main floor, and off that was the kitchen. All of the residential quarters were at the back of the house.

I rushed down the hall, poking my head into each room before I got to the door that separated the private living area from the rest of the premises.

"Birdie?" I knocked. Waited.

"Birdie." A bit louder.

No answer. She probably couldn't hear me.

There was a key around the doorframe somewhere, but for the life of me, I couldn't locate it. I decided to head back and find out what Fiona had to say. The fact that neither she nor Lolly seemed at all concerned had me wondering if perhaps Mrs. Honeycut had had a nightmare and if my vision was something I would catch later on an episode of *Castle*.

Back in the parlor, the couple was seated on an antique settee, Fiona perched on a chair in front of them. Apparently, she was next in line to try to communicate with Mrs. Honeycut. I didn't see Deirdre or Leo, but I did spot Lolly measuring the back of John's head. She was about to fit him with a top hat when I intervened. There was an empty chair next to the fireplace, so I parked her there and poured a healthy shot of Jameson from the cherrywood bar.

Mrs. Honeycut was making a valiant effort to put a teacup to her lips. The saucer was sloshing liquid all over her lap, but that didn't seem to bother her.

My aunt was speaking in hushed tones. After a few minutes, Fiona looked at John.

"She's ready now." Fiona relieved Mrs. Honeycut of the cup and saucer, patted her knee, and nodded.

I eyed the cup, wondering just what was in that tea.

"Okay, folks, let me get the Chief in here and you can tell him what happened," John said.

He walked to the door and yelled, "Yo, Leo!"

I tensed. I hadn't seen Leo in a week and I missed him. I was also still a little pissed.

Leo walked in, raising the temperature of the room instantly. He was wearing my favorite jeans that cupped him where I used to and the leather jacket he never zipped. His panther-black hair dusted his dark eyes and there was a little more stubble on his chin than usual, which made him tastier than ever.

"Hi," he said to me. "How's the shoulder? The leg?"

"Healing," I said.

He nodded. "Good. Good."

Leo crossed to where the couple sat and introduced himself, showed them his badge. "Can you tell me what happened, ma'am?"

Mrs. Honeycut took a deep breath and I noticed her face had been wiped clean.

"Well, I was preparing to retire for the evening," she began slowly, then paused.

Leo nodded, looking very concerned, and Mrs. Honeycut seemed to loosen up even further. He had that calming effect on women. Well, most women.

"And my husband was in the sitting room while I changed into my nightclothes."

Next to her, the man confirmed this with a nod of his head. He smiled at me, then winked. There was no time to contemplate that before a shrill cry cut through the air.

Mrs. Honeycut jumped. Everyone else looked at me.

"Sorry," I mumbled, backing from the room. I pulled out my cell and checked the text.

It was from Monique.

COME GET YOUR BRETHREN BEFORE I TOSS HER DOWN A WELL

Dammit, Ivy. There was no time for her crap. I texted Monique back and told her I'd be there ASAP.

Before I even turned back around, the scent of sandalwood told me who would be standing there.

"Why do you sneak up on me like that? I hate that!" I said.

My grandmother eyed me up and down, crossed her arms, then arched a perfectly tweezed eyebrow. She was taller than me, which made for masterful intimidation. It almost always worked.

"It's about time," she said.

I could have taken that a number of different ways, but I chose to ignore all of them. One family crisis at a time.

I said, "Your guests are in the parlor with Leo. Something upset them and it's not the usual kind of upset, like 'I thought I would be meeting three sweet old ladies and instead I spent a weekend with the Witches of Eastwick.' It's a bit more dramatic than that." I didn't tell her I couldn't stick around to find out what the problem was.

"Hmm." She paused theatrically. "Well then, we shall converse later, Anastasia."

That nickname was fun for about five minutes.

Birdie's gypsy garb fluttered and chimed as she floated toward the parlor, her red cape billowing behind her. I followed, preparing to make a left turn for the doorway.

That was when I heard Mrs. Honeycut say, "Dead. Right there in the bathroom."

To which Birdie replied, "Impossible. That wasn't supposed to happen until tomorrow."

There was a brief silence, and then Mrs. Honeycut gasped and said, "It's you. I saw you out the window earlier. Holding a dagger!"

Well, this might take longer than I thought.

Chapter 23

IVY GERAGHTY'S PERSONAL BOOK OF SHADOWS
by Ivy Geraghty

Entry #7

I am patiently awaiting further instructions from the blood of my blood, flesh of my flesh, my sister, Anastasia. Meanwhile, I study the Enemy closely, crafting my plan to identify, target, and align her adversaries into our camp, for the Enemy of my Enemy is my friend. (No idea who said that, but I'm pretty sure it was some Asian philosopher because I saw it in a fortune cookie. Scully thinks it's a righteous citation.)

—Ivy Geraghty, Junior Apprentice Warrior Goddess (in training)

Chapter 24

"So you're telling me that this is a murder-mystery weekend and all your guests were given a part to play in it?" Leo asked.

"Actually, not just our guests. Several other hotels and inns are participating," Fiona said. "There's a dinner later down at the Riverview Hotel."

We were all standing upstairs in the hallway just outside of the old couple's room.

"But I don't understand," Mrs. Honeycut said. "We never heard a thing about it."

Mr. Honeycut chimed in. "This weekend was a gift from our daughter." He turned to his wife. "She must have forgotten to mention it, Cece."

Fiona said, "The instructions for the game should have arrived along with your reservation confirmation."

Mrs. Honeycut was beginning to look like one of those old cat clocks with the roaming eyes and nervous tail.

"But you"—Mrs. Honeycut turned to my grandmother—"I saw you with a knife in your hand. Just outside the window. I recognize the cape."

Why was Birdie wearing her ritual cape anyway? There was nothing special about tonight, no holiday. Nothing she would have cast a spell for. And even if there were, she would have done it in the back of the house, near the woods—not on the front lawn, where her guests might intrude upon the magic.

Birdie gave the crowd a long-suffering look. "I'm afraid you are mistaken, Mrs. Honeycut. It wasn't a knife or a dagger in my hand at all. It was a garden trowel. I was simply clearing out a bed to prepare for the spring thaw. Tomorrow will be an unseasonably warm day and the lavender could use the sunlight."

I shot Birdie a hard look. Now I was confused. It wasn't yet Ostara, the spring equinox, which is when she cleared her beds. Plus, the lavender was on the opposite side of the property. I had planted it myself.

What was going on? I felt my brow crinkle and immediately smoothed it out. When I looked away, Leo was staring at me.

Mrs. Honeycut wasn't convinced, so Leo said, "Why don't I take a look just to be sure. With your permission, of course."

She nodded and Leo tapped on the door to their quarters. It creaked, hesitated, then yawned open.

A pear-shaped man with a hooked nose stood in the sitting room. He had a towel in his hand and what appeared to be blood all over his yellow plaid shirt, topped off by one of those prop knives that appeared to go straight through his neck. "Don't tell me the game is over already," he said. "I was just practicing." He eyed Mrs. Honeycut. "You really know how to scream, little lady. I almost thought that was real. You might just win the grand prize if you keep that up."

Mrs. Honeycut grasped her husband's elbow and slunk back.

Fiona stepped forward. "Mr. Sayer, what on earth are you doing in the Honeycuts' suite?"

"Honeycut Suite? I thought this was my room," he said, and looked at Lolly. "She gave me the key."

Lolly adjusted her necklace and said, "Oh my, I'm so sorry." She looked at Birdie, worried. Apparently Lolly hadn't had enough booze in her at check-in time.

Birdie put a hand on her sister's shoulder. "These things happen, dear."

The sound that escaped from Leo was something between a sigh and whimper. John cackled.

"C'mon, Chief, I'll buy you a beer," John said.

"Hey, can I come?" asked Mr. Sayer.

I didn't hear their response because I was halfway down the stairs, off to retrieve my brethren.

The wind had picked up. It was the kind of cold that slaps your skin and seeps into your bones just to remind you to appreciate the spring. I jogged all the way to Down and Dirty, trying to outrun it.

The high-pitched screech of Madonna's "Like a Virgin" wailed through the speakers as I opened the door.

The club was dark, so I stood for a moment, eyes adjusting. A cocktail waitress holding a tray filled with test tubes approached me, clearly on a mission.

"Hey, you want a shot?" Her liquid soldiers clinked together, then came to a standstill when she did. She was going for the big-haired MTV look.

I shook my head.

"Oh, I think you do," she said.

Looking past her, I strained to search for Ivy.

"No, I'm good, thanks." I stepped to the side of her tray.

"Can't come in unless you do a shot." She put an arm across the entryway, blocking me from going forward.

For a moment, I considered cracking her over the head with her own tray, but that was more my cousin's style.

"Why the hell not?" I asked.

She rolled her eyes and glanced over her shoulder.

"Look, it's not my call. It's my first night and the boss says no one gets in without an eighties costume unless they buy a shot."

Of course. And I had no money.

I said, "Cindy." It was on her name tag. "I am in costume. Can't you guess?"

She stood back and looked me up and down for a minute. I sure hoped she'd come up with something, because I hadn't a clue what this black ensemble could qualify as in the costume department.

Slowly, I saw the wheels turning as she tried to form a picture in her mind. Her brown eyes lit up. "Oh yeah." She smiled. "But where's your mask?"

"My mask?"

"Don't the Teenage Mutant Ninja Turtles wear masks?"

I mentally slapped her and moved on.

The crowd was thick with middle-aged drunk people reliving their John Hughes moments. I didn't see Ivy anywhere and couldn't hear a thing over what I now realized was a karaoke machine with Monique at the wheel.

"'Like a vir-ir-ir-irgin, touched for the very first time!'" She was shimmying up and down a pole, screaming into the microphone, but really all she could do was wave her arms because the mermaid skirt was wrestling her legs and wasn't about to let go. She reminded me of a worm wiggling on a hook.

Scully was hunched over the bar in his usual spot, so I approached him, asked where Ivy was.

He was sipping a beer, staring down at a piece of paper that he promptly folded. There was a purple string tied around his wrist.

"Haven't seen her," he said.

"Really? So you often tie purple strings around your wrist, do you?" That had to be from a spell charm.

His eyes flickered briefly, then he pulled his sleeve down.

"What's on the paper?" I asked.

"Nothin'."

"It better not be what I think it is." If Ivy was practicing magic in this wide-open venue—with booze flowing and people running in and out and no stable energy concentration—it could only lead to trouble.

"She's a good kid. Don't you go yellin' at her," he grumbled.

Scully had been a fixture in this town all my life, and I don't believe he had said that many words to me in total, let alone all at once.

"I'm just trying to protect her," I said.

He lifted his eyes with warning. Ivy must have told him about our dispute the last time she came here. Then he sees her again unsupervised, and that mixed with the fact that she probably bought him that beer he was drinking (which was highly illegal and enough ammo to use against Monique should I need any) seemed to have worked together to forge some sort of odd bond. The only things I had ever seen Scully show any concern for was his barstool and his beer.

He scowled and thumbed to the back room.

"Thanks," I said.

I decided now wasn't the time to worry about the friendship between my newfound sister and Amethyst's oldest resident, so I shoved that to the back of my mind and stepped into the back room.

The scene came at me in quick snapshots. Ivy. The cards. The bloodstone. It was in the center of the table, vibrating with such intensity the sound reached me ten feet away. Rage propelled me forward and I grabbed her forcefully.

What I didn't see was who sat across from her.

Chapter 25

Bloodstones are powerful, and that power is difficult to harness. They are audible oracles that hum when charged and open gateways to our ancestors and spirit guides. Symbolizing truth and justice, they were called the Warrior stone by ancient soldiers who wore bloodstone amulets to protect them from fatal wounds.

Which was perfect, because I was about ready to kill this kid.

"Ow! What's your issue?" Ivy asked.

"What's my issue? Are you kidding me? I thought you had more sense than this." I pocketed the stone—my stone, by the way—and reached for the tarot cards.

"Those are mine!"

I didn't bother to face her as I collected the well-worn cards. How long had she been at this? Tarot reading was not on the Geraghty syllabus. If it didn't come from within—if the magic wasn't something you could see, touch, or feel—it was not respected or trusted by Birdie. "Not anymore," I told her.

Then I saw the money and my blood turned to lava.

My eyes met hers and held them. "Are you hustling?"

Ivy grew very quiet.

"Answer me, Ivy. Right this minute."

"No." She looked down at her shoes. "I just tell fortunes and do little good-luck charms. You know, to practice. Sometimes people pay me for it."

So that was where she got her bankroll.

I threw my hands up. "Next you're going to tell me there's a Ouija board in your backpack!"

"There is not! I'm not stupid, you know."

I took a step forward, wishing I could wave a wand and make her realize how dangerous a game she was playing, but a strong arm pulled me back.

"Take it easy, kitten."

Leo only called me that when I was under extreme distress. Unfortunately, that was more often than either of us would have liked.

He turned me around and regarded me like I was wearing a bright shiny bow he wanted to unravel.

For a minute, nobody spoke. When I got my bearings I said, "Oh, so now you understand about this stuff? Do you have any idea how old she is?"

Leo's lips turned just at the corners, apparently amused at my frenzy. "Your little sister did mention that she's not yet old enough to drive."

Ivy spoke up then. "I told Leo about how we met in the program?"

I looked at her, puzzled. What the hell was she talking about?

"I think it's great you joined Big Brothers, Big Sisters," Leo said.

So now we were stealing, hustling, and lying. Tomorrow, we'll be making moonshine in the bathtub.

Ivy's face pleaded with me to keep her story straight, so I said nothing. Why was she hiding our sisterly secret from everyone but me? Granted, Chance knew because we had to crash at his place, but why no one else?

Thankfully, John swung around the corner then and shoved a bottle of beer in Leo's hand. "Hey, it's the cat burglar," he said.

"Aren't you supposed to be on your honeymoon?" I asked.

"Yeah, well, you kinda spoiled that, didn't you? Anyway, Deirdre's firing up the karaoke machine," he said. "That Sayer fella talked her into a duet."

The bars to "Summer Lovin' " crooned through the speakers then.

"Oh, Stacy, can I sing next?" Ivy asked.

Suddenly, I understood how Leo must have felt dating my family and me. Reality challenged, every last one.

Exasperated, I said, "Do you not understand what's happening here? What you've done?"

She shrugged. "I get it, you're mad. You'll get over it."

John laughed, and I backhanded his shoulder.

He didn't flinch, but he did point out that assaulting a peace officer was a felony. Naturally, Leo chimed in with the time he arrested me for launching a snowball at his cruiser.

Ivy said, "You've been in jail? That is so cool."

"It's not cool and it's not what you think. I'm about as threatening as Mary Poppins."

"Didn't Mary Poppins ply kids with sugar and make them fly off the roof?" John said.

"Why are you here again?" I said.

Leo explained that John had been his mentor many years ago back in Chicago. Now he investigated judges, which is how he'd met Deirdre. She was a court stenographer.

"This guy was your mentor? Really?" I asked, and Leo just smiled.

Monique made a Herculean effort to two-step through the doorframe then, carrying a shot that she handed to John. "For Deirdre," she said.

Her seashell bra must have been exceeding the manufacturer's recommended capacity because the ladies were pointing in two different directions, clearly trying to escape.

"You owe me a dance, Officer." She looked right at me, put her arms around my former man, and stuck her tongue down his throat.

It took everything I had not to kick her fin out from under her.

The storm of the century was brewing back outside. That's another quality of bloodstone—it wreaks havoc on the weather. Call a cab, call Chance, or walk?

"Why didn't you just punch her?" Ivy asked after a minute.

"Why would I do that?" I said, but I was really thinking, *Yeah, why didn't I?*

"It's so obvious Officer McHottie has it bad for you, and she is a total tartlet. I would have sunk her to the ground." Then she did some swift martial-arts move that was most impressive.

"Boy, are you going to like Cinnamon." Luckily, my cousin was due back tomorrow.

I couldn't wait for Cinnamon to get home. I missed her but I also had a suspicion that she could relate better to Ivy than I could. She wasn't that much younger than me, but she was craftier in the violence and high jinks department.

"And he's not a Mc-anything. He's Greek." I looked down both sides of the street. Not many people around, and no one I knew to ask for a lift.

"Well, whatever he is, I wouldn't mind having one of those with a side of Chance for breakfast. Except, you know, *my* age," she said. "How did you get so lucky, anyway?"

"It's a small town." I fumbled through my pocket for my phone.

"I mean, I think you're super pretty in a Maybelline-ad sorta way, but still, two scrumpalicious boys at the same time?"

Found the phone. "What? No. I'm not dating either of them." No signal. Damn.

The scent of rain was in the air and, as cold as it was, it would probably freeze on its way down. That would not feel good on the skin.

Ivy continued to babble. "They both want to date you, I can tell. You should play the field, live a little. Make them jealous. You know, when I was in the eighth grade, Heather Hutchinson—have you ever noticed all Heathers are blonde? Anyway, Heather liked Bobby and—"

"Stop! Why the sudden interest in my love life?" That's when I noticed she was rooting around in her backpack.

I narrowed my eyes. "What are you doing?"

"Nothing." Ivy shuffled her feet.

"Hand it over."

"Fine." She passed the backpack over to me and I looked inside. Something was glowing.

"What is that?" I asked.

The door to the club opened then and Leo said, "Do you two need a ride?" Just then, a wide vein of light divided the sky, followed by a thunderous jolt.

"Sure!" Ivy said, and winked at me.

"No," I said.

"Come on, you'll catch pneumonia out here," Leo said. "Car's right across the street."

Ivy bounced over to it and said, "Do you know where Chance lives?"

Leo looked at me like I had just stolen his lunch money, but I didn't worry about that on the ride home. If he could let Monique slobber all over him, then I could sleep with (or near) anyone I wanted to.

I did, however, worry about what was in Ivy's bag that glowed.

Chapter 26

"I would have picked you up." Chance looked over my shoulder at Leo's car.

I gave him a look that left no room for further discussion on my choice of transportation.

Ivy stretched and yawned. "I'm sleepy. Time for me to hit the sheets."

"Why don't I tuck you in?" I followed the little red fireball.

Ivy backed away slowly. "Nah, I'm a wee bit too old for that, sis." She grabbed the backpack and made it just toward the first step that led to the basement. Chance was watching, a bemused smirk on his face.

I stepped forward. "I think maybe I should stay downstairs with you. First night in a new place and all. You might have bad dreams." It was a warning, and the flicker in her eyes told me she knew it.

Ivy tried to rush off, but I called Thor, who was a better linebacker than anyone on the Bears. He bounded up the stairs, puffed up his shoulders, and anchored his rear onto the landing. He grumbled something of an apology to Ivy, then trained his gaze on me.

Chance said, "I'm going to bed. You two have fun." He walked over and gave me a peck on the cheek that sent a surprising sizzle down my neck.

Chance disappeared upstairs and Ivy turned to glare at Thor. "I gave you my Cheetos. I thought we were pals."

Thor whinnied and shrugged but didn't take his eyes from me.

"Downstairs," I ordered both of them.

Thor yawned and stretched, then ambled down the stairs and crawled on top of Ivy's bed. He circled three times and plopped down, his huge head nestled in a pillow, watching us.

Ivy flipped the light on and tossed her bag on the bed. "Go ahead and search," she said.

That was too easy. What was she up to? I felt uncomfortable searching her things. If it were me, I would want the opportunity to explain.

"Why don't you just tell me what it is you don't want me to see?"

"Promise not to get mad?"

"Nope."

She rolled her eyes. "It's the money. There's probably more than you would expect." She started talking faster. "Look, I didn't know how long it would take to find you. I had to survive somehow. No one got hurt and I didn't cheat anyone, I swear."

For the first time since we met, I looked at her like the frightened child she was. The barely-a-teenager-would-be-orphan.

I was her once. Except I had family around me. Support and love. Ivy was alone. She knew this wasn't a game. I could see it all over her. She wore confidence like a cloak, but that was purely a defense mechanism. She had to pretend this *was* a game, because at the moment she had no idea where life was leading her.

I sat down on the bed next to her and held her hand. "I'm not mad about the money. You're safe now, okay?"

She nodded, sniffled a little.

"Tomorrow, you and I are going to have our first lesson."

Her eyes grew bright with excitement and she began to speak, but I stopped her. "With Birdie's supervision," I said.

"But why? You're the powerful one."

Where was this girl getting her information? "Maybe I am and maybe I'm not, Ivy, but I have never been a teacher. I've never passed my knowledge along, and since you seem to have learned just enough to be dangerous, we need to lasso and tame your talent before someone gets hurt. Agreed?"

"Agreed."

"Now tell me what was glowing."

"I already did. The money."

"Why was the money glowing?"

Ivy slid off the bed and bent over to unlace her boots. "It's one of those pens that bankers use to make sure bills aren't fake. Mom worked at a bank for a while, so that's how I know. If the bill is real the ink turns yellow. I guess it glowed beneath those neon bar lights." She kicked off her boots and stretched. "I wanted to make sure no one in the bar ripped me off, so I scanned them with the pen."

She bewildered me every day, this one. I had witnessed Cinnamon run a marker over larger bills at the Black Opal on occasion, presumably for the same reason. "What would make you think that someone would pass you a fake bill?"

Chance had left a T-shirt folded on the dresser. Ivy examined it, held it up to her chest, and frowned at the Steelers logo. She slipped into it anyway. "I don't know. It happens. Mom talked about phony money sometimes when she was on the phone."

It was strange to hear her talk about my mother in the years after she had left Amethyst. It left me feeling empty. Discarded.

Like phony money.

I stood up and Thor opened one eye. "I guess I should get ready for bed too." I walked over toward the light switch and Thor jumped down.

"Stacy?" Ivy said. "Would you mind—just for tonight—sleeping down here with me?"

I turned around and said, "Why not?"

Four hours later, I knew exactly why not.

Chapter 27

The guttural growl of a nearly two-hundred-pound dog awoke me from an empty dream. Thor's head was low, targeting something small in the corner of the room. Slowly, I raised my head, then my shoulders, and tried to focus my eyes.

I couldn't see anything around Thor's body. A quick glance at Ivy told me she was sleeping soundly and smiling.

Then all hell broke loose.

Something chattered and squeaked and leaped through the air to land on the dresser. Thor roared and darted across the room, but whatever the flash of gray was, it was much faster than Thor. Faster even than my sight could follow.

Then Ivy's backpack bumbled and danced around the dresser top, and I figured that whatever the thing in the room was had burrowed inside her bag.

Amazingly, the kid was still asleep. Still smiling.

Thor threw a glance my way and I gave the hand signal for him to heel. He trotted around the bed and stood still by my side, ears erect, tail straight up in the air. I lifted the covers, extracted one leg after the other, and slowly stood up, rubbing the sleep from my eyes.

Ivy giggled and rolled over, still in dreamland, and the thing popped its head out from the bag. I couldn't make out what it was, but it chirped little bird noises and its eyes were green marbles.

There was something in its hand with glowing slash marks all over it. Thor tensed and released a long, threatening growl. The thing held whatever it was in the air—a bill from Ivy's cash wad, maybe—squawking and pacing back and forth along the dresser.

From the bed, Ivy mumbled, "Petey," and the thing on the dresser dropped what was in his hands, flew across the room, hovered above her for a split second, then floated to a wall shelf.

Thor flashed his canines and targeted the shelf. In one impressive leap, he took it and several of Chance's old baseball trophies down to the carpeted floor in a thunderous wave.

Ivy bolted awake and screamed. I ran for the light and flipped the switch.

There was nothing but a puff of smoke where the flying creature once was.

I stood there in silence, stunned. Even Thor was quiet, but it was just we three in the room. Then Ivy said, "Was Petey here?" just as Chance came rushing down the stairs.

"I heard screams. What—" Chance halted at the edge of the stairs as he surveyed the damage.

I rushed toward him. "There was a mouse and Thor got a little overzealous chasing it. I'm sorry." I shot Ivy a glance, and she nodded.

"Sorry," she said.

Chance walked over to where the shelf had been attached to the wall, tracing the hole with his hand. He put his fingers through his hair and sighed. "It's not too bad. I can patch it." Then he turned toward us. "You're both okay, though?"

"Fine," I said, and he shook his head and shuffled toward the stairwell.

After I heard the door shut at the top of the stairs, I turned back to Ivy. "Who is Petey?"

She pulled her knees to her chest and said, "He was my first stuffed animal—a squirrel—when I was a baby. I slept with him all the time. We lost him once in a move. Sometimes I think about him and I can see him."

I stared at her for a second, then told Thor to go to sleep. He curled up by the foot of the bed and I stepped into the bathroom to wash my hands and gather my thoughts.

This was more than I could handle, I knew that now. I needed Birdie's help—like yesterday. First thing in the morning we would head over there, possibly stay at the inn if there was room. We had to tell her everything. Birdie had every right to know that her daughter might be in danger. And that she might have another grandchild.

The sink was filling up with water but I hadn't plugged the drain. I twisted the faucet and went fishing for what was causing the blockage. The stopper put up a fight but it finally relented and popped out with a clang, clang, clang.

Only it wasn't the stopper that made the noise. It was a penny. The year I was born.

I padded back to the bedroom. Ivy was already on her side of the bed and I slid in beside her. I set the alarm for six a.m., enough time to talk to Birdie before she served her guests—and prayed for a dreamless sleep.

The last thought that ran through my mind before I drifted off was, *If that thing was what I think it was, I am in way over my head with this kid.*

Chapter 28

IVY GERAGHTY'S PERSONAL BOOK OF SHADOWS
by Ivy Geraghty

Entry #8

Today, I shall meet the mother of my mother, Brighid Geraghty, descendant of the Great Goddess Brighid, whose fire still burns on the Green Isle in the county of Kildare. (Although I think it's completely asinine to roll out of bed at the crack of dawn.) At the home of my mother and her ancestors, we shall combine the talents of two generations of Geraghty women and continue our quest to save one of our own.

—Ivy Geraghty, Junior Apprentice Warrior Goddess (in training)

Chapter 29

"Ivy, hurry up in there. We have to get to the house before breakfast," I said through the bathroom door. Saturday breakfasts were a little more hectic than Sundays. Guests were usually in a rush to get downtown for shopping and sightseeing. Not only did we need to talk to Birdie, but also I needed to get my hands on the book. Where had Fiona stored my things?

The trophies and the shelf were stacked in a corner of the basement, and I dusted up the crumbled drywall and tossed it in the trash. There was a note for Chance on the kitchen counter telling him where we would be, and the pennies were tucked in the tiger's-eye locket that hung around Thor's neck. I was showered and dressed and in desperate need of coffee.

I sat on the bed and reached for my black boots, thinking about the thoughtform from last night.

A thoughtform (also called an egregore) is a manifestation of energy created through visualization. They aren't real beings but often take on an anthropomorphic or zoomorphic form. They serve as watchers, messengers, even companions. It takes a good deal of concentration and practice to develop one, and only the most powerful and well-honed witch can charge a thoughtform.

Never have I heard of anyone who could do it in her sleep like Ivy had done with Petey.

The door clicked softly and Ivy emerged from the bathroom all sleepy eyed. She yawned and said, "It's practically still dark outside. Why on earth do we have to leave so early?" She yawned again and fumbled through her backpack. She pulled out a black ball cap with a white pentagram embroidered on it and cupped it on her head, tucking her ears under, then straightened her fiery mane. She walked over to give Thor a belly scratch.

"Because the guests are served at eight o'clock, and the sooner we get this over with, the better." I ushered her toward the door.

We made it to the inn in under ten minutes. There was no sign of life in the front of the house, but I was certain there was some food preparation happening in the kitchen.

If only that were all that was happening, things may have turned out differently.

Chapter 30

The view through the glass panes in the door showed Mr. Sayer slumped across the apothecary table that served as the prep island, a dagger sticking out of his back and blood staining his shirt. For a split second, I panicked, but then I remembered he was taking this whole murder-mystery weekend seriously—although I suspected his cover was blown at that point.

The spare key was kept in a gargoyle's mouth that guarded the flower beds. I liberated it and unlocked the back door. Ivy followed.

"Stacy, I have to use the bathroom," she said.

There was no sign of Birdie or the aunts.

"Down the hall to the right."

She scampered off and I greeted Mr. Sayer. He stuck to character, not uttering a word, so I crossed to the marble countertop near the old Hoosier cabinet to pour myself a cup of coffee. The sun was peeking through the window over the farm sink when Aunt Fiona emerged from the back stairway a few minutes later. Lolly trailed behind her.

"Oh, hello, dear. You're up early." Fiona was so put together for this ungodly hour, one might suspect she had a crew working on her all night while she slept. Lolly, on the other hand, had decided to set her hair in pin curls. Using actual safety pins. She looked like a voodoo doll experiment gone horribly wrong.

Lolly shuffled, head down, toward the countertop where the mug tree dutifully carried all the coffee cups on its sturdy wooden arms. Fiona reached for a bottle of Bailey's Irish Cream as Lolly contemplated which mug should set the tone for the day. She chose one with a caption that read, "Life's a witch and then you fly."

Birdie emerged from the fruit cellar then, two jars of homemade jam in her hands—raspberry, or perhaps strawberry, and peach. Most of what they served their guests was either harvested from the gardens on the property or supplied by local farmers.

"Anastasia. What a surprise." She said it like it was anything but. "Come to help us with breakfast?"

I held up my coffee cup in a gesture of greeting. It had been a gift to me from Birdie years ago that I never packed up when I moved out. It read, "My grandma can put a spell on your grandma."

"Sure."

She nodded, then turned to the apothecary table to relieve herself of her load. She glanced over at Mr. Sayer and grunted. "For Pete's sake, is he still at his silly game?" She picked up the not quite empty mug next to Mr. Sayer, placed it in the sink, and crossed to the cast-iron stove, where she turned the oven dial to 350 degrees.

"Guess he really wants to win that prize," I said, sipping my coffee. "What is it, by the way?"

Birdie waved her hand. "Who knows? There's some dinner down at the Riverview Hotel, and that's where the festivities will take place this evening." She pulled out a pan from the refrigerator. Stuffed baked French toast, from the looks of it, with blueberry filling. Then she said, "I don't know why I let the Chamber members talk me into such nonsense. It only serves to attract the lonely and the unbalanced."

The Geraghty Girls' Guesthouse attracted that clientele every weekend, but I didn't say that. Instead, I reached for a warm-up and wondered where Ivy had gotten off to and how exactly I might introduce my grandmother to her new granddaughter—or if she would even believe Ivy's story.

I ran a few introductions over in my mind as I watched Fiona dice fresh fruit compote to accompany the French toast. *So Birdie, guess who has a sister?* Or perhaps, *"It's a girl!"* might be the way to go.

"Stacy, be a dear and please wake him. He must have fallen asleep or passed out. I have no time for shenanigans during the breakfast hour." Birdie put the French toast pan on the counter to let it reach room temperature. Then she climbed back down the steps to the fruit cellar.

I set my coffee down and said, "Mr. Sayer? Rise and shine. It's almost breakfast time."

He still lay there, like a growth that had sprouted from the wood. I stepped forward and said louder, "Come on, I'll help you back to your room and you can practice being the murder victim later."

He didn't stir. In fact, he was silent.

Really silent.

My stomach did that flippy-floppy thing it did right before I heard Mrs. Honeycut's scream. The vision flashed again, piercing my head with nothing but red. Blood red. The chair caught my sway and I stilled myself.

Fiona was humming as she chopped the fruit. A Gershwin tune. "'You like tomato and I like tomahto…'"

I looked closer at Mr. Sayer, or more accurately, the knife standing on his back, which seemed uncomfortably familiar.

"Fiona, does that, er, blade handle look like anything you've seen before?" I asked.

She turned around, looked at Mr. Sayer, and frowned. "I suppose it might be a plastic imitation of the ritual athame your grandmother uses."

I stepped closer to Mr. Sayer. Maybe he was just a really good actor with the air capacity of a zeppelin. I saw no movement coming from any part of his body. Statue stiff.

My voice cracked as I called, "Birdie…did you see Mr. Sayer earlier this morning?"

"I did. Did you get rid of him yet? Can't have any stray bodies lying around." She sounded irritated, still banging around down the cellar steps, mumbling about purple potatoes.

I had to be mistaken. Had to be. A corpse in the kitchen would be really bad for business. "What, um, exactly did he say?"

Fiona looked up from her chopping. Arched her swan-like neck.

"Honestly, Anastasia, I don't have time for this," Birdie called.

After a moment of shuffling noises, she still hadn't come back up the stairs, so I ducked my head down.

"Humor me, Birdie," I said.

One exasperated sigh later, I heard her say, "If you must know, he didn't say much of anything. He came home smelling like a brewery last night and asked me to pour ketchup on his back. Said he was really enjoying the game. I must have forgotten to latch the door after I went back into the kitchen. I found him there drinking coffee this morning. Your aunt Lolly had a time of it last night, what with all the excitement, so she needed her rest and I didn't have the energy to chase him out."

Lolly was the primary chef. It kept her out of trouble and Birdie away from the guests first thing in the morning. Birdie didn't mind cooking, but she did mind strangers in her kitchen, and no matter how many notices you post, people will wander where they aren't supposed to at a bed-and-breakfast. She once caught a group of people—not even guests—who had come in off the street while she was in the garden. They were looking for a place to stay, and since they were told Amethyst was such a friendly community, decided to help themselves to a vintage merlot. I don't know what she slipped into the open bottle as she explained there were no vacancies, but I didn't see those people anywhere in town the rest of the weekend. Or ever again, for that matter.

Fiona smiled widely and made a gesture like she was wiping sweat from her brow.

I walked over to Mr. Sayer and gently shook his arm. "Mr. Sayer?"

A trace of lavender floated directly behind me. Fiona was at my back. She put a hand on my shoulder and gave it a squeeze.

"He's not moving," I said to her. "Feels just a bit cold."

"Well, it isn't yet spring. The air is still sharp."

We both looked at Lolly, who grinned back, took a hit of Bailey's Irish Cream, and began unpinning her hair.

I said, "Okay, let's go with that."

Birdie emerged from the cellar, a jar of honey in her hand. "I cannot find the purple potatoes." She looked to me, then Fiona, and said, "What?"

I spoke. "He isn't moving, Birdie. Not even his chest. You know—where the air comes in."

Birdie rolled her eyes. "Oh, please. He's fine. Probably just passed out. See if he has a pulse. I have to dress." Then she floated up the back stairwell.

Fiona nudged me, and I briefly wondered how I got stuck with the job of pulse checker for the family business.

Gently, I peeled back the collar on Mr. Sayer's shirt, then hesitated.

"What is it dear?" Fiona asked.

"His shirt is damp."

Fiona leaned over my shoulder to get a look.

Behind me, I heard Ivy say, "Whoa, dude was a vampire snack."

I snapped my head around and looked at Ivy standing in the doorframe that led to the dining room.

"There are no such thing as vampires." I glanced at Fiona for clarification on the matter, because honestly, how the hell would I know? "Right?"

"That's right, dear," she said.

Then the front doorbell rang, and since I couldn't think of a worse time for Ivy and Birdie to meet, I sent her to answer it. Luckily, Fiona seemed more concerned with the issue at hand than about Ivy, and the Bailey's had yet to kick in for Aunt Lolly.

When there's a dead guy in the kitchen, everything else seems much less important.

Chapter 31

IVY GERAGHTY'S PERSONAL BOOK OF SHADOWS
by Ivy Geraghty

Entry #9

The power that radiates from the house of my ancestors is electric! I can feel it everywhere, and I know in my heart of hearts that the blood of the Goddess from whence we came still flows through my body generations removed. My grandmother is an inspiration to witches everywhere and especially to me, as it will be my first encounter with an High Priestess of the Old Ways. I have much to learn before I am initiated into the coven, but study hard I will and the Mission shall continue. (Except there's a stiff in the kitchen who is seriously crunching my mojo.) Now I shall see who calls on the house of the Geraghtys.

—Ivy Geraghty, Junior Apprentice Warrior Goddess (in training)

Chapter 32

After a quick phone call to the police station, I darted out the back door and around to my cottage.

John's hair was unkempt and his shirt inside out as he stumbled to answer my knock. No sign of Deirdre. I quickly explained the situation and asked if he would come check it out, since I was, after all, just a newspaper reporter and not a doctor. However, given the condition of Mr. Sayer, I was doubtful an ambulance would help. I was trying to buy Birdie and the aunts a bit of time and save their guests from waking up to sirens. Hopefully, they could send the wagon, or whatever they call the vehicle that picks up bodies, around to the back of the property without disturbing the guests.

Fiona prepared a cup of coffee for John while Lolly wandered into the dining room. I heard the clang of silverware a few seconds later as she set the table.

As if a guest dropped dead every day before the timer on the oven buzzed.

John scratched his head and leaned in to smell the man's shirt. "Who poured ketchup on him?"

I nodded toward my grandmother.

John looked at her and asked, "Why?"

She sighed. "He asked me to. Yesterday evening. I can't believe he's wearing the same shirt." She was checking on the baked French toast and didn't turn around.

John snapped his fingers and said, "Oh yeah, that murder-mystery thing." Then he circled the table, squinting at the body slumped across it, and scratched his head again. Fiona offered up the coffee and he thanked her.

"Tell me again why you didn't call Leo." This directed at me.

"I did. Gus told me he was out on a call and he would send him over ASAP. Said he would let him know what was going on."

"Did he say how long he would be?" John took a big swig of java, eyeing Birdie.

"He just said Mr. Shelby called to report someone had altered his goats again," I told him.

Fiona sighed and shook her head. "The poor dears. What was it this time?"

I shrugged. "Something about writing 'Go Eagles' in block letters on a dozen of them."

John looked like someone had just poked him in the forehead with a sharp stick.

I tried to explain, although really, it didn't make much sense to me why people harassed those poor goats. Last time, they had been smeared with Nair. "The high-school basketball team has a good shot at making it to the state finals."

I continued, "I really didn't want Gus to be first on the scene." Gus made Barney Fife look like Sherlock Holmes.

"Plus, I was hoping to avoid a marked car parked out front so the guests wouldn't be frightened. I thought maybe you could help sort things out until Leo can get here."

John sucked down more coffee. "You should have just called an ambulance. They'd pick him up in a small town like this."

"So...is he? Dead, I mean?" I asked.

Fiona said, "Perhaps his heart attacked him?"

I looked at Mr. Sayer, who was on the far side of fifty. He could have seriously benefited from a gym membership.

"What about around his neck? It's wet," I said.

John held out his cup, seeking more caffeine, and Fiona obliged. "Deirdre accidentally spilled her drink on him when they were singing karaoke. No telling cause of death without a coroner's exam." He looked at Birdie. "Mrs. Geraghty, if you don't mind, just run through it for me step by step. When did you first see Mr. Sayer in the kitchen?" He pulled a stool out from beneath the table, flipped it around, and straddled it backward.

Birdie was draining bacon on a paper towel. She explained that Mr. Sayer was sitting in the same stool he was in now when she arrived down the back stairs. He had already helped himself to coffee. She greeted him and went to work on preparing the morning's meal.

John stopped listening halfway through the story. He was close enough to Mr. Sayer that he could lean his head over the man's back. Then he blinked a couple of times, sat back, frowned, and said, "You want the good news or the bad news, ladies?"

Chapter 33

"What's the good news?" I asked not really wanting the answer.

John crossed his arms. "The good news is he won't be annoying any of you or your guests anymore."

Lolly chimed in, excited. "What's the bad news?"

We all stared at her for a moment, and John said, "Not sure he died of natural causes."

I shook my head. "No, no. That can't be."

John rose to his full height. "Stacy, there is some blood on his shirt. That may not be a prop knife, but I'm not going to touch it to find out." Then he frowned. "Although there isn't as much blood as there should be if he were stabbed." He looked at Birdie. "Mostly it's ketchup."

Suddenly, Ivy was very noticeably absent. Panic bubbled in my stomach. What was taking her so long at the door? The thought of a knife-wielding maniac prowling the house jump-started my legs into action.

"Okay, everyone take a deep breath. I'll be right back."

I ran down the hallway before anyone could protest, ducking my head in different rooms, thinking maybe Ivy had gone exploring.

I found her in the parlor, seated across from a young couple dressed in their Sunday best. The woman wore a modest floral number buttoned up to her eyeballs, and the man was in a green sport coat, tan slacks, and a wide-brimmed hat.

Ivy was chatting away cheerily and I sighed in relief. Such a good helper. This must be the last reservation and she was making them comfortable.

"Hello there. Sorry to keep you waiting. Are you checking in today?" At this point, I wasn't sure what the plan was, so I decided to just stick to the usual routine. There was nothing in *Bed-and-Breakfasts for Dummies* that explained dead-guy protocol.

I hadn't really noticed the expression on either of their faces up until that point. The woman stood, hurried to me, and the man stayed in his seat, staring at Ivy with worry. And fear.

The woman pasted on a bubbly smile and glanced back, nervously. "Hello. My name is Edna and this is my husband, Richard. This, er," she stammered, sweeping her arm toward Ivy, searching for a proper adjective, "lovely young lady was kind enough to invite us into your home. We were wondering if you might have a few minutes to chat with us."

I heard the man say to Ivy, "Crystals, dear, are not what saves us."

Uh-oh. I did a quick inventory of the situation. Ivy was wearing that pentagram hat that the uninformed often viewed as a symbol for dark arts. It can be, if the top point of the star faces downward, but her hat was embroidered with a typical pagan pentagram. Used in many rituals and ceremonies, the pentagram represents the elements of earth, air, fire, and water, and, finally, the point at the top of the star stands for the sacred spirit.

Even if she had explained this to our guests, I doubt these two would have heard.

"You have a lovely home," the woman was saying. "Perhaps we might have a cup of tea and we can show you all the literature we brought? This child seems eager to learn about Jehovah."

Ivy had a wicked grin on her face. "I thought maybe we could share *our* literature with them too, Stacy." She was flipping through a magazine titled *The Watchtower: Questions for Young People*.

I used to send Birdie to the door to handle these situations. But after the last time, when two Mormon missionaries left the church, rented an apartment in town, and started a hip-hop band, Birdie wasn't allowed to speak to anyone spreading the word of Jesus. Or Jehovah. Or even Hare Krishna.

Ivy said, "I was telling them that we believe in Watchtowers too and—"

"Okay, kiddo. I got it," I said to her. To the woman standing next to me I said, "I'm terribly sorry, but you see we are very busy at the moment. As you may know, this is a bed-and-breakfast and we are right in the middle of preparing the morning meal. So if you'll excuse us..." I looked at her hopefully.

"Oh, well, perhaps your guests would welcome the opportunity to discuss a chance at true happiness," she said.

"True dat!" Ivy clapped.

I glared at her and through gritted teeth said, "I don't think that is appropriate."

The man stood and took a step toward me then and asked, "Do you feel a knocking at your heart, child? Like someone is calling to you? That is Him asking to be let in."

I felt a knocking in my head, like a migraine with my name on it, but that was about it.

"I hear it," Ivy said.

"Stop it, Ivy!" I snapped.

The man shook his head in sorrow. "Wouldn't you want to live in a world where there is no conflict, no grief, no sickness?"

Sure, but there's a stiff in the kitchen with a knife in his back, so why don't we take this up tomorrow?

That's what I wanted to say, anyway, but instead I went with, "How about this. You give me your address and we'll drop by at a more convenient time. Say around supper? Then we can go through every single pamphlet you have. We'll make an entire evening out of it."

The woman looked at the man and said, "Oh, well, I'm not sure that is the best idea."

He looked confused and said, "Perhaps not, no."

"Of course it isn't!" I said. "Because no one wants a stranger dropping by her home unexpectedly at mealtime. What if there isn't enough pot roast? Even Jesus had limited seating." Kind of regretted that last part, but I was pretty stressed out.

I heard a car start then and rushed to the window. Birdie's Cadillac was peeling down the driveway.

Dammit!

"Ivy, please show Edna and Richard out and give them a coupon for Pearl's Palace. Best fish fry in town," I said to them. Then I rushed back toward the kitchen.

Chapter 34

IVY GERAGHTY'S PERSONAL BOOK OF SHADOWS
by Ivy Geraghty

Entry #10

I have endured my encounter with Those Who Fear What They Do Not Know. I relish a second opportunity to Enlighten them in the spirit of the ways of old. For there is not one path that carries us all. Each must find her True North (okay, I snagged that one from Oprah, but she's like the closest thing to a Goddess here on Earth). I wait for further instructions.

—Ivy Geraghty, Junior Apprentice Warrior Goddess (in training)

Chapter 35

My stomach launched an all-out campaign to be fed as soon as I got back to the kitchen. I could only assume it was the salty aroma of real bacon that had it in uproar.

Lolly had that look that said her mind was about to take a coffee break. When she stuck her finger in a blueberry muffin to determine if the batch was done, I had my confirmation. She pulled out a gooey blue mess and I grabbed an oven mitt. Given the situation, I guessed the Bailey's wasn't cutting it.

"Aunt Lolly, why don't you take a break for a minute?" I guided her to a chair in the dining room and helped her sit down. Popped the muffins back in the oven and turned to Fiona.

Mr. Sayer was still in his seat but I didn't see John. "Where's John?" I reached for a tablecloth from the upper cabinet and covered Mr. Sayer with it. Seemed like the right thing to do.

"He went outside to phone that nice boy Leo to tell him your grandmother was heading down to see him at the police station. So impatient, Birdie is."

"What?"

Lolly squealed and tossed a dishrag over her head.

"Keep your voice down, please."

I apologized and Fiona gave me a curious look. "I don't know why you don't give Leo another chance. He's got a good job, a nice personality, and great buns."

Seriously? We're going to have this conversation *now*?

Deep breath, Stacy. Deep. Breath. I reached for the bottle of Jose Cuervo and said, "I don't like this, Fiona, not one bit. I cannot believe you let her go." Why would she go? Why not wait here?

I poured Lolly a shot and slid it across the table. "I'm heading over there."

Fiona laughed. "Nonsense. Your grandmother knows what's best." She scooted around me and said, "Isn't that right, Lolly?"

Lolly bobbed her head and downed the spirit.

"There, you see?" Fiona reached around and turned the oven off.

"And this?" I pointed to Sayer.

Fiona looked back from the open oven door. "He'll be taken care of shortly. John said he would ask Leo to send some sort of team right away. Now, be a dear and help me finish setting the buffet."

"Fiona, you cannot serve breakfast in the middle of a crime scene."

"That's what John said. Wanted Lolly and me to stop everything we were doing and leave the room. Imagine, telling me what to do in my own home." She shook her head. "Not feeding people when they are hungry—that would be a crime. Besides, it's all prepared. We just need to get the food and beverages into the dining room, and then I will see that the kitchen door stays latched."

There was no arguing with that kind of logic.

I grabbed the platter of bacon and the scrambled eggs and headed into the dining room.

"Who is all this food for, anyway? There are only four people to feed."

"No, dear. We also have a very nice group of girls. That's why we put the honeymooners in your cottage. The girls are sharing the suite."

I decided to bite my tongue on that decision for the moment, since she had enough to contend with. Fiona put a finger to her lips in thought as I set the eggs down. I reached into the top drawer and pulled out a doily. Presentation was everything in this house. I unfolded the doily and as I did, a vision hit me.

A tall figure leaning over a desk. Hands flipping through a book. My stomach lurched and a feeling of dread exploded in my chest.

I put the plates down and kissed Fiona on the cheek. "I gotta go, Auntie."

"What? What about breakfast? I thought you were going to help?"

She looked absolutely bewildered, and I hated leaving her with all the work, not to mention the inevitable investigation, although I suspected Lolly would be coming around any minute. I couldn't explain why I had to rush off. Not then, anyway.

Ivy. Ivy would have to do it. She was a strong, smart kid, I doubted serving breakfast to a quiet group at a B&B would trip her up. I would just tell her to go with that same story she told Leo. That she was in a Little Sister program at the community center. It would have to do until I could properly explain the situation to the aunts and Birdie.

"It's covered." I grabbed my coat. "And please, reroute it to the parlor, would you?"

I had to get to my grandmother. I smelled trouble. Mixed with bacon. And tequila.

Chapter 36

Dispute not with her: she is lunatic.
—William Shakespeare, *Richard III*

I explained things to Ivy, who apparently was a fan of the movie *Tombstone*, because she said, "I'll be your Huckleberry."

It wasn't until I got outside that I remembered I still had no idea where my stuff was, and that included my car keys. Or rather, the keys to my grandfather's car. Mine was still in the shop after taking a nosedive into an icy lake. Birdie had her car, so it looked like I was walking.

I had my gloves on and was at the third step when I heard, "Don't think so."

John was walking up to the porch.

"I don't have time for your bullshit, John." I continued down the steps.

He put his hand out and said, "Look, for some reason Leo thinks you're the sane one in this nuthouse, so he asked me to make sure you stayed put until the team got here."

I laughed. "John, fewer people live in this town than were in your entire graduating class from high school, I'm sure. The 'team'"—I used air quotes—"consists of a few uniformed officers, a three-legged labradoodle, and until a couple weeks ago, my eighth-grade biology teacher."

"You gonna give me a hard time? Leo warned me you have a tendency to look for trouble."

I rolled my eyes and nudged him aside. It took him about two seconds to cuff me to the porch railing.

"*Not* funny. Uncuff me."

John laughed. "Soon as the boys get here."

I ran my hand up and down the rail, hoping to loosen a spindle. "Agh!"

"Yep. They sure don't make houses like this anymore." John slapped the railing.

Deirdre called for him then and John said quietly, "Believe me, kiddo, this is not my idea of a honeymoon. Just doing a favor for a friend."

He jogged down the steps and around the corner.

"Damn you, Leo," I muttered.

The front door creaked open after a couple seconds and Ivy poked her head out. Without saying a word, she shot forward, reached into her backpack, pulled out a key, and slid it into the lock. She disappeared back behind the front door just as fast.

She was like an anime character. I wondered what else was in that backpack as I jogged to the police station.

Gus Dorsey was the first person I saw when I walked through the doors. Gus has had a huge crush on my cousin, Cinnamon, since high school, but since his thighs are about as thin as fettuccini and his ears could take flight at any moment, it was never a mutual attraction.

We think of him as Deputy Dawg. He thinks he's Clint Eastwood.

He was playing with one of those paddleballs and he couldn't keep the thing in the air for more than two whacks. There was a stun gun in his holster where an actual gun should have been. I'm not clear as to the true version of the story, but it was rumored that Gus had shot himself in the ass about a year ago. I didn't want to think about how that was even possible.

He chased the ball down the hall just as the door swept shut behind me.

The entryway of the station house was divided in half by a short, wooden wall, a swinging gate the only barrier between the lobby and the dispatcher. I didn't recognize the woman behind the counter. She must have replaced Betty, which was okay by me. Betty had a lot of laughs at my expense. Mostly due to my unfortunate knack for stumbling across dead bodies.

At least this time, I wasn't the one who found it first.

"Hello," I said.

She raised a finger to let me know she'd be with me in a minute. She seemed to be fielding a call about a UFO sighting.

"That big, eh? Hovered right outside your window, you say? Was it round? Uh-huh," she said. She was in her sixties, plump, bouffant hairdo, and press-on nails. Her reading glasses were attached to a thin chain that was lost in the cleavage of her pink sweater.

"Okey-dokey. Say, did you get Violet's invitation? Yep. I know. Her kids look more like that neighbor than her husband." She cackled and a snort escaped.

"Excuse me?" I said, louder this time.

Yet again, she held up one expertly pressed-on nail longer than a carving knife.

"Oh, sure, yeah, that could be. Uh-huh."

I tapped my foot to keep myself from planting it in her ass.

She sent me an unapologetic look and continued her conversation. "You know, I don't doubt it. I think I've seen one myself. Oh, sure."

Then she had the nerve to spin around, her back to me, and put a foot up on the half wall.

"Big as the moon it was. Yep."

There was a bell on her desk that said "ring for service," so I did. Repeatedly.

Ding! Ding! Ding! Ding! Ding!

She sighed with disgust. "Hold on a minute, Martha."

"Stop that now. Can't you see I'm on the phone? Where are your manners?" she snapped, dangling the receiver.

"Is that a citizen complaint?"

I could hear Martha bust out laughing on the other end. Miss Press-On spat into the receiver, "Did you hear that, Martha? As if you would make an official complaint!" Pause. "I know. Can you believe the nerve?"

In a small town, stories take on a life of their own. Needless to say, there are several versions still floating around Amethyst regarding what happened next. In my defense, my mother was apparently missing, I had just found out I had a sister, there was a dead guy in the kitchen of my grandmother's house, and I had skipped breakfast. But I would like to go on record stating that I have never struck a woman twice my age.

I pounced on the desk and yanked the phone from her chubby hand. She jerked in surprise, and with her foot on the rail, the shift in weight sent the chair wobbling. She shrieked as I put the receiver to my ear and said, sweet as sugar, "Hello? Martha? Yeah, she'll have to call you back." Then I slammed the phone down.

I filled my lungs with air and said, "Now, I would like some assistance, please."

Her bottom lip quivered, but the chair was coming to a halt. She looked at me in horror. "Gus!" she shouted over her shoulder. She didn't take her eyes off me.

Gus strolled up to the desk then took one look at me and bolted.

"Gus! You little weasel! Get back here!" I shouted.

Miss Bouffant swiveled her head from side to side, not sure what to do.

"I'm going in," I said to her.

She nodded.

I swung through the little gate and ran around the corner, full throttle. Unfortunately, I smashed into Leo and bounced off him like a bullet off Superman's chest.

"Jesus! Are you okay?" He asked, bending down to help me. "I heard Stella calling Gus. Thought something was wrong."

"Thank you." I stood, stepped away from him. "Why isn't he at the B&B right now anyway, collecting evidence or at least getting in the way of someone else collecting evidence?"

"I asked the sheriff's department to partner on this one. The county medical examiner would have to process the body anyway, since the coroner passed away."

Leo must have seen that I was upset, because he didn't offer a lecture on my choice to leave Birdie's house after a guest had permanently checked out. He also didn't ask how I'd escaped a man twice my size. With handcuffs.

"Your grandmother is down the hall. She's just finishing up her statement. Come on." Leo put a hand on my back, guiding me through a long corridor.

"Don't touch me."

He dropped his arm.

"You didn't have to come down here, Stacy. You know she's in good hands."

I knew she had a big mouth.

I said, "She should have a lawyer."

"For what? She isn't accused of anything, and from what John told me, my guess is the guy got in a bar fight, got a little blood on his shirt, passed out at the kitchen table this morning, and had a heart attack. He was still tipping the drinks when we left. I saw the stunt he pulled yesterday with that knife through the neck, so my guess is he was still at it this morning."

"You think so?"

Leo gave me a warm smile and nodded. "Birdie insisted on coming down here to personally tell me everything she knows. Probably to keep me away from you."

I don't know how it happened, but an irrational bitch took possession of my mouth. "Well, can you blame her?"

Leo turned to me, his upper lip curved in that way it does when he's confused. "What exactly is your problem? You broke it off with me, remember?"

The bitch wasn't backing down. Now she had control over my hands. She wagged a finger at Leo. "And *you* just couldn't wait to climb aboard that silicone-stuffed herpes ride, could you?"

"What the hell are you talking about? *You* are the one who shacked up with your old boy toy about five minutes after you dumped me!"

"*Enough!*"

We both turned to face Birdie. I hadn't realized we had made it all the way down the hallway. Crap, did she hear that last part about shacking up with Chance?

She relaxed her face, straightened out her blouse, and gave us both "the look." "I should think that two grown adults who claim to have cared for one another at some point could have a civilized conversation without getting into a shouting match."

Oh, please. The woman has been divorced for thirty years and still uses my grandfather as her personal tongue sharpener.

"Sorry," Leo grumbled.

"Suck-up," I mumbled.

Birdie cleared her throat.

"I mean, sorry," I said.

"Better. Now, come on. I don't have all day." She held the door open and we both entered the room.

Leo pulled a chair out for me and I sat down. He took a seat across from me and Birdie settled in the chair next to me.

Leo glanced down at the paperwork, read through it. "Mrs. Geraghty, I think I have everything I need here from you. Look it over one more time before you sign." He slid the page across to her. "The rest of your guests and your sisters will be questioned, of course, and if by some long shot the knife—plastic or otherwise—turns out to be the cause of death we can just take your fingerprints, rule them out, and that should clear things up on your end." He looked at her. "Please, next time something unusual happens, just wait for us to get there."

Birdie ignored that part. "You will handle this with discretion."

Wasn't really a question.

Leo said, "You have my word that we'll do our best. We'll need to sweep the room Mr. Sayer booked and hopefully find some contact information to notify his family." He handed Birdie a pen.

"May I see the statement?" I asked.

Birdie passed the paper to me.

Leo said, "If you want, we can take your prints now and we shouldn't need to bother you further."

"Oh, they're on file." I regretted the words immediately. He may never have had to know that. Leo sat back. "They are?"

Birdie sighed. "Yes, apparently test-driving an automobile is a crime."

"It is when you drive it out of state," I said.

Her voice gained an octave. "I had to take it on the highway. How else to know if a car runs well?"

"For six hours?"

Leo stood up, "Okay then. I think we're done here."

I was still scanning the statement. Birdie had said earlier that Sayer had helped himself to the coffee, but here it just indicated there was a coffee cup in front of him when she entered the kitchen. She assumed he was playing dead again. She didn't mention sticking a prop knife in his back, but how could he have done that himself? And how could it have stayed there if it was just a prop knife? Unless he took his shirt off first and glued it to the fabric. Her version stated that she didn't recall seeing the knife until Fiona and I pointed out that he was still in her kitchen.

I looked at Birdie, who stood, ready to leave, and decided to ask her a few questions myself in private. Like, had she left the kitchen at any time? Perhaps she had made a trip into the fruit cellar before I got there? That might have given someone enough time to slip into the kitchen undetected.

The phone buzzed then and the gate guard with the press-on nails said, "I have someone on the line here for Stacy Justice."

I checked my phone. No bars. Ironic, I know.

"His name is Chance," she said.

Leo slid back noisily and stood up. "I'll see you out, Mrs. Geraghty." He walked around and whispered in my ear. "I'm not seeing her. She kissed me to get under your skin."

"Didn't work," I lied.

He flashed a look I couldn't read, then guided Birdie out the door.

I had no intention of telling him his assumption about Chance was anything less than accurate. Let him wonder.

I picked up the receiver and punched the blinking button.

"This is Stacy."

"Hey, Stace. Your phone was going right to voice mail and Fiona said you were at the police station. Everything okay?"

I really didn't want to get into the whole scenario at the moment, so I told him it was.

"Listen I...found something." His voice had an edge to it. Nervous? Excited? "You better come to my place quick. Bring Ivy too."

Chapter 37

IVY GERAGHTY'S PERSONAL BOOK OF SHADOWS
by Ivy Geraghty

Entry #11

I have received word from my sister to meet her back at our hideout. What is the urgency, I wonder? Has she located the Blessed Book? Has she uncovered a sinister plot that involves our mother's kidnapping? I make haste on foot (and not a moment too soon, because I'm pretty sure the big white ride outside isn't a limo for the living. I mean, RIP and all that to the dude, but the creep factor is off the charts on this one, even for me).

—Ivy Geraghty, Junior Apprentice Warrior Goddess (in training)

Chapter 38

I texted Ivy, asked her to meet me at Chance's place, then hurried from the police station. I didn't see anyone on my way out, and when I searched the parking lot for Birdie, I discovered she hadn't bothered to wait. That was okay by me, frankly. There were still unanswered questions floating around my mind. Like, why had she rushed to the police station? Was Sayer animated when she first saw him? How often had she left the kitchen? But I feared she had a few questions for me too, and since I wasn't ready to explain the lie about taking a trip, nor was I ready to explain Ivy and my missing mother, I decided it could wait.

The sun was bright, melting the snow into muddy puddles as I walked to Chance's house. My leg was beginning to throb from the wound—the wound courtesy of a crowbar-wielding maniac. Just when I was wishing I had a car, Derek Meyers, the photographer for the *Amethyst Globe*, pulled up alongside me.

He rolled down the driver's window and leaned his dark, unlined face out, the wind not altering his tight hair one bit.

"You want a ride to the office?" he said.

"I'm on leave, remember? Injured reporter here. But I will take a ride." I hopped in the passenger seat and my leg thanked me by slowing the pain to a steady ache.

Derek turned the car off, draped his arm over the seat, and stared at me, both eyebrows raised. We hadn't known each other that long, but our professional relationship and the newspaper business in general required a certain amount of mutual respect and a fully functioning bullshit detector. The look on his face told me Derek's was cranked all the way up to high.

Crap. He knew something. But what? Which absurd event that had dropped in on me these past few days was he aware of?

I read an Einstein quote once that said something like, "The only reason for time is so that everything doesn't happen at once." I'd bet a million dollars Einstein had never met a Geraghty, because from my vantage point everything was most certainly happening at the same time.

When the life of any of my loved ones or my own life is under direct threat of imminent danger, I'm usually fast thinking and, I have to admit, quick-witted. This was not one of those times.

"What?" I said stupidly.

"You gonna sit there with your big green eyes and try to make me think there isn't a posse parked out by your granny's house with a big ol' meat wagon front and center?"

"Really? I had no idea." That was kind of true, actually. Those poor guests had had no idea what they were in for when they signed up for the murder-mystery package. Probably they would never leave their homes again.

I craned my neck as if I could see through the thirty houses that separated the block we were on from Birdie's corner.

With a snap of my fingers, I said, "You know, there is that murder-mystery thing this weekend. That's probably it. They're making it look authentic. Can you drop me off on Ruby Lane?" I asked, not a hint of concern in my voice.

"Not until you tell me who died."

I sighed. What was the use? He would find out soon enough anyway. "Look, all I know is he's a guest at the inn and his last name is Sayer."

"Cause of death?"

"Do I look like the coroner?" I was getting a little agitated. Of course I was going to work the story, but until I had more information, there wasn't much to report.

"Well, come on, woman, give me something. Was it at least suspicious? Did your granny poison his pancakes or something?"

Anger took control of my mouth before my brain could gag it, mostly because I hated the word *granny*. "Drive the damn car, Derek!"

Derek's lower lip dropped a little bit. "I was kidding, Stacy, but don't play with me. If there's something going on, you gotta clue me in."

The problem was, I didn't even know what was going on at that point, but I suspected soon I would have to come up with something to bring to Shea Parker, my editor, and with the other "family" problems I had to attend to, Derek might have to partner with me on this one. He would have his work cut out for him interviewing the Geraghty Girls, but I knew he had more ambitions than snapping photos for our small paper, and he was hungry for the opportunity to investigate a story.

It didn't take long to realize that I needed Derek to have my back on this one. His assistance meant I could steal some time to look into what had happened to my mother—a story newsworthy for the *Amethyst Globe* as well, although one I would never share with any other reporter. I'm sure its founding father—*my* father—would agree with me on that point.

Maybe it was time to give Derek a break after all.

"I'll give you everything I know once I know it."

Derek shook his head. "Uh-uh. Not good enough. You cut me in from point A."

I sighed to make him think *I* was doing *him* a favor. Mostly because it would be easier to get him to follow instructions, but also because I couldn't have him going rogue. He would have to check in with me every step of the way because—Goddess forbid—if there was something rotten in the house of Geraghty, I needed to know about it before the rest of the world.

I promised him a co-byline and he started the car.

When we got to Ruby Lane, I told Derek I would text him to let him know when we would meet. Then I called Parker, my dad's old business partner and my boss, and left a message asking if he was available to come to the office today. Parker texted back, said he was making chili and *how about noon*? I agreed, forwarded it to Derek, and knocked on Chance's door.

Before he answered, my cousin, Cinnamon, sent a message that she was on her way home from the airport and couldn't wait to see me. Said she had a surprise.

I didn't bother telling her that I had a few surprises myself and agreed to meet in the afternoon at her place.

If Chance had told me on the phone what he had discovered, I never would have made any of those plans.

Chapter 39

Chance swung the door open before I reached the stoop. He looked a bit harried and his face was moist as if he had been working out, but he was wearing a tight navy T-shirt rather than the usual sleeveless jersey he wore to pump iron.

"Hey, how did everything go at Birdie's?" he asked.

I said, "Let's talk about it later. What did you find?" I didn't see Thor. "And where's my boy?"

"Out back with Ivy." Chance grabbed my hand and said, "Come on. It's downstairs."

I tried to ignore the jolt of electricity at his hand engulfing mine as I trotted behind him down the stairs to where Ivy and I had slept last night. The back door opened and coos of Ivy sweet-talking Thor drifted down to us.

"Ivy, come downstairs and shut the door to the basement, please," Chance called.

The shelf was reattached to the wall, the trophies back in place, and the bed made. Guilt sucker-punched me.

"Chance, I would have helped you put the room back together," I told him.

"Stacy, I'm a contractor. It was no big deal." He looked at me, lowered his voice, and said, "I'm sure you can think of a way to make it up to me."

I elbowed his shoulder and Ivy bounded down the stairs.

"Did you tell him, Stacy?" Her face was flushed as if she had run all the way here.

I shook my head, widening my eyes to indicate I had not and didn't plan on it right now, thank you.

Ivy just nodded and feigned a hangnail.

Chance was busy fiddling with a lamp that was on the shelf. Either he hadn't heard her or he chalked it up to nothing important.

"Chance, what did you call us down here for? What did you find?" I asked.

He reached for the shelf and produced the article Ivy had found in the purple box. The article that had brought her to Amethyst. To me.

"One second." Chance smoothed the page out on the bed, adjusted something on the lamp again, and asked Ivy to run over and wait by the light switch until he signaled to turn it off.

Patience was something I should have acquired years ago, growing up with Birdie and her theatrics, Fiona and her love potions, and Lolly and her...well, just Lolly. Somehow, though, the trait eluded me.

"Dammit, just tell me!"

I am working on it, though.

"Geez, keep your pants on." He smirked as he said that, then he said to Ivy, "Now."

She flipped the switch and the room blackened except for our eyes, our teeth, and Ivy's hat.

All of that was glowing.

"This is what you dragged us down here for? A black light?" I asked.

"Retro," Ivy said.

I would have gone with creepy. "Chance, 1987 called and said they want their light back, and P.S.—chicks *do not* dig it."

Ivy jumped in. "Actually that was a conference call with 1974, and they want their lava lamp back."

Chance stiffened next to me as Ivy and I laughed. "Would you two just look, please." All I could see were his eyes narrowing.

"Are you pointing at something? Because if you are, I can't tell," I said.

"The bed." His teeth gritted as he spoke. That I could see.

I looked down at the bed and saw a series of slash marks atop a slip of paper. The article. The article I wrote was on the bed. Someone had marked it up in code with glowing ink.

"Ivy, this was what was glowing in your backpack! Not the money you marked with the counterfeit pen."

I thought that ink didn't glow. I had used it at the Black Opal enough times and that place could get awfully dark after last call. The article was what I saw that glowed—and even pulsated.

Kind of like it was doing right now.

The letters appeared to be coming at me in 3-D. I looked at Ivy. She was staring at the note. Did she see that? Did Chance?

Chance said, "I have no idea what kind of code that is, but it has to be some kind of message, either to Ivy or you, Stacy."

"It's Greek to me," Ivy said.

The letters seemed to float off the page. Danced around me. Every word composed of simple slash marks. Some diagonal. Some straight. There were circles too, which I could only guess were highlighting the words or letters in the actual text of the newspaper article. It would be tricky to decode and time-consuming, but I knew it could be done, and had to be done fast.

"Ivy, run up and grab my laptop."

She bounded up the stairs.

One word popped out at me. The only one my brain could instantly translate.

Because I had seen that language before.

The word was *ivy*.

Chapter 40

IVY GERAGHTY'S PERSONAL BOOK OF SHADOWS
by Ivy Geraghty

Entry #12

Oh joyous day! A hidden message. A secret code. Finally! A step closer to uncovering The Truth. Watching my sister work her magic sends shivers down my spine. (Pretty sure Chance feels the same way, but Stacy is, like, sooooo oblivious.) I bring Sister her trusty tool for cracking codes. (Okay, so it's not The Book. It's a computer, but whatever.)

—Ivy Geraghty, Junior Apprentice Warrior Goddess (in training)

Chapter 41

Ivy had left the door open when she went up the stairs, and Thor sauntered down, trotted over for an ear scratch, then curled up near the heat vent. The light from upstairs was chasing away the darkness as I turned to Chance.

"Thank you and your black light," I said.

"You know, chicks did dig it once. My dad told me so." He grinned.

I grinned back. "They also dug mullets. Things change." He knew I was teasing him and he chuckled. That was the thing about Chance. He was never threatened by women. Overprotective at times, at least with me, but never threatened.

I had forgotten how easy it was to be with him. How much fun we used to have together. After I moved back and began dating Leo, I kept my distance from Chance. Out of respect for both of them and because I didn't want to send mixed signals.

I missed his friendship.

Ivy fluttered down the stairs, flipped the light switch, and said, "Got it!" Burst my thought bubble just in time.

There were more important things to worry about right now than my love life.

Like what the hell the message was trying to tell us.

"So do you know the code? Do you know what it says?" Ivy was so excited she was bouncing, her long hair flipping up in ribbons. Thor caught her excitement and hopped over to lean against her. He nearly knocked her over as he looked from Ivy to Chance to me, waiting for someone to explain what all the fuss was about.

"It's written in Ogham—an ancient language of the Druids," I told her. "It was named after Ogma, the Celtic god of eloquence."

"It looks like what I've seen on rune stones," Ivy said.

I nodded and turned on my laptop. "The structure of the letters is similar, yes, but runes are typically Germanic. The Celts never used rune stones for divination." I looked up at her. "But they did use this."

Chance said, "You mean this is a magic language?"

The laptop was still booting up next to the note on the bed. I looked at Chance, pointedly. I had never been all that comfortable with the word *magic*, or at least the present-day connotation of the word. As Birdie had taught me, magic is simply the culmination of energy and will.

"It was a secret, *ritualistic* language used in the fifth and sixth centuries across Celtic lands. Sometimes for spell casting, sometimes in divination or to call the gods, but also to pass messages. It was so secret, in fact, that the alphabet was guarded by priests and scholars alike. When they needed a written record of something, they used Greek letters. Confused the hell out of Julius Caesar, who assumed the Gauls felt the written word was taboo. He wrote about it in his *Commentaries on the Gallic War.* Of course, the real reason was to protect Ireland from the Romans, which Caesar never did invade."

Chance said, "They certainly didn't cover that in my history class."

"You didn't attend Birdie's after-school specials," I said.

I keyed in my password.

"So how do you read it?" Chance asked.

I explained that on the page, Ogham is read from bottom to top and the twenty-five letters represent sacred trees and plants (hence the word *ivy* popping out at me).

"It's also a sign language." I pulled up Google and tapped the keys.

Ivy read over my shoulder. "The Book of Ballymote. Is that like the Blessed Book of the Geraghtys?"

"Sort of." I told her the story.

The Book of Ballymote was written in 1390 or 1391 inside Ballymote Castle in County Sligo, Ireland. Commissioned for Tonnaltagh McDonagh for his own clan, the book was compiled by Manus O'Duignan, Solomon O'Droma, and Robert McSheedy—prolific scribes of the time.

The book was a compilation of historical events—such as the life of Saint Patrick, the history of the Jewish people, Christian kings, and the fall of Troy. It was also embedded with valuable documents like the Book of Invasions and the Book of Rights, the triads, genealogies of important Irish clans and kings, maps of the land, a history of Celtic women, poetry and prose (including a copy of *The Aeneid*), and of course, the Ogham alphabet and language.

The book itself has had quite a history. For over a hundred years, it remained in the possession of the McDonaghs of Corran. It was then stolen by a member of the O'Donnell clan, where it stayed until the Flight of Earls in 1603. The manuscript was then lost until 1620, when it was donated to Trinity College in Dublin. It sat in the library there until thieves stole it once again in 1767. Eighteen years later, it resurfaced in Burgundy, France, and made its way back to Ireland, where it was preserved by the Royal Irish Academy.

"Makes you wonder what was in there that was valuable enough to steal," Chance said.

I had never thought about it before. That book sure made its way around the Continent.

"They finally made copies of it in the late 1800s, but I think the original is still in the hands of the Royal Irish Academy."

Ivy read over my shoulder again. "It says here that the work opens with a drawing of Noah's ark, but the first written page has been lost."

"Huh," Chance said, "that's interesting."

"Very interesting," Ivy agreed.

"Let's focus on the task at hand, kids." I climbed onto the bed and situated the computer in front of me. I asked Chance to grab a notebook and a pen and told Ivy to turn out the light. They both then sat across from me on the bed, Ivy's notebook in her lap.

We had three hours before my lunch meeting to decipher the note, and I didn't want to waste it wondering about a missing page of an ancient text from another clan. However, one fleeting thought occurred to me before we began.

Where was *our* book?

Chapter 42

My phone vibrated as we were finishing up. The clock on the computer read 12:02.

I rose from the bed and stretched. Chance must have noticed me wince because he asked if I wanted some aspirin. I did.

Ivy went to get us some water and I checked my phone. A text from Birdie.

I am waiting, Anastasia.

Leave it to my grandmother to make an appointment and not inform me. She never asked me to meet her back at the house, or anywhere, for that matter. What was she waiting for?

Chance dropped two aspirin in my hand and asked when my stitches were coming out.

"Oh crap," I said. "Birdie was supposed to remove them today after breakfast." Oops. Guess that was what she meant.

Ivy handed me a bottled water and I downed the aspirin.

"Why don't we move to the kitchen table?" I suggested.

The process of interpreting the note was tedious on the brain and a strain on the eyes. Each symbol in the Ogham alphabet stands for a letter that also represents a tree or plant. For the ivy vine, it's one vertical slash with two horizontal lines across it, like a plus sign with an extra slash. So to interpret it, we needed to figure out the letters that made up the words, find the words that were circled in the English text, put them all together from bottom to top, then reorganize the structure so that it made some sort of sense.

If we screwed it up, we'd have to start all over again.

Ivy and Chance had both taken notes as I read the letters off. Now we just had to combine the two.

Except I had about three appointments to attend today, and the first one began five minutes ago.

"Chance, do you have a job today?" I asked.

He shook his head and I pulled him aside.

"Would you mind keeping an eye on Ivy? I have to go into the office for a little bit and then get my stitches out, but I shouldn't be more than a couple of hours." I hoped.

I still needed to find out where Fiona had stashed my things and especially get the Blessed Book. There had to be some clue in it about all this. At the very least, maybe I could cast a spell to call on Maegan in a scrying session. Surely she would have some answers.

"Sure, I guess. But what about this?" He pointed to the pages of notes and the article spread across the counter.

"The hard part is over. Ivy can put it together, I'm sure." I squeezed his shoulder. "Maybe you can help?"

"Puzzles are more my little brother's thing than mine," he said. "But I'll give it a shot."

I didn't want to push my luck, but I had a lot of running around to do today. "Can I borrow your truck?" I smiled wide and said, "Please. I'll take good care of it."

Chance eyed me suspiciously. "Your Jeep ended up in the bottom of a lake not too long ago, Angel Eyes."

"That wasn't my fault. I almost never drive my car across thin ice."

He sighed, scratched his head, and reached around my waist for the key ring on the counter. He dangled the keys in front of my face briefly, leaned in close, and whispered in my ear. "Try to make it home in one piece."

"I'll take good care of your baby. Bring it home without a scratch, I promise."

Chance held my eyes. "I wasn't talking about the truck."

He brushed his lips against mine, briefly, then backed up.

I caught Ivy watching us. "I have to go out for a little while. Think you can complete the decoding, Ivy?"

She saluted me. "Piece of cake, sista." Then she snapped her fingers and said, "Hey, can I tell him about—" Her eyes slid to Chance. "You know."

I assumed she was referring to the unfortunate demise of Birdie's guest this morning. "Knock yourself out." I called for Thor and we headed for the door.

Just before I closed it, I heard Chance say, "Who brought the cat?"

Chance has a monster of a truck, so I felt pretty safe once I got inside. But something was off, something felt… naked. A quick glance around made me realize I had none of my talismans with me.

Since the fire, I had made sure I had a little protection stashed in every corner of my life. At the cottage, there are two sardonyx stones guarding the entrances to prevent crime. A clear quartz dangles from my rearview mirror for safe travels, and my office drawer has a sachet of angelica seeds, mugwort, and horehound. There's even a vial of rose geranium oil in my gym bag, not to mention jewelry in every gemstone you can imagine in my jewelry box.

Right now, though, I didn't even have my amethyst necklace. I did have Thor, however, who was wondering why we weren't moving yet and told me so by bellowing long and loud. The dog lived for car rides.

That's when I noticed he was still wearing the tiger's-eye locket with the pennies inside.

Tiger's eye has been worn for protection for centuries. It's known to ward off curses and fight any form of dark magic. It also protects our four-legged loved ones.

I unclipped the gemstone from Thor's collar and said, "I'm just going to borrow this for a while, buddy. Soon as I can get to my own things, you'll have it back." Thor agreed to the arrangement by nibbling my ponytail, and I started the truck.

Two cars I recognized as Parker's and Derek's were in the lot when I pulled up to the news office. The key to the building was on my key ring, wherever that was, so I had to buzz the front entrance for them to let me in. I waited for the buzz-back sound while Thor assaulted a shrub.

No buzzing sound came.

I pressed the button again. And again.

"What the hell?" I muttered.

The back door was a steel number, but I tried it anyway and got nowhere. I noticed a light from inside the second-floor conference room on my way back around to the front door. Was it on a minute ago? I couldn't be sure. Maybe the intercom was broken?

I sent Parker and Derek each a text.

U there?

I waited.

No response. Perfect.

I circled the building one last time, Thor trailing behind.

That's when I saw it.

A spider's web over the back door. It was a big sucker too. My stomach was sloshing like a roller coaster and fear gripped me.

Uninvited guest.

Thor barked. He was standing in front of the stone wall that wrapped the building. It was just high enough that I might be able to peek in the window.

Maybe it was nothing. Maybe they were talking to a citizen about a lead. Maybe someone saw them pull up and they invited him in for chili.

Anything was possible.

The boots had some good traction and it was only one floor up, so I thought, *How hard could it be?*

Anyone who has ever had a sadistic gym teacher who brought out that stupid rope to climb knows—it's pretty freaking hard.

After I slid down the wall for the third time, breaking every single fingernail in the process, I finally figured out that Thor was hollering at me. I turned to see him standing in the bed of the truck. Which, of course, made much more sense than pretending to be Spiderman.

Barbra Annino

It's a humbling moment when you realize your dog is smarter than you.

I hopped in Chance's truck, drove it around, climbed in back with Thor, and we both jumped from the cab to the wall.

When I looked in the window, I screamed.

Thor acted.

Chapter 43

IVY GERAGHTY'S PERSONAL BOOK OF SHADOWS
by Ivy Geraghty

Entry #13

Message received! I, Ivy Geraghty, Warrior Goddess (that's what Mom always called me anyway. I know about six forms of martial arts that end in "do." That's right—I can kick ass in any language), have decoded the secret message left by my mother. This is too important to wait. We must move fast, for the Enemy is closer than we think. I rush to my sister at once!

—Ivy Geraghty, ~~Junior Apprentice~~ Warrior Goddess (in training)

Chapter 44

Great Danes are sensitive dogs, highly attuned to human emotions. If you scold them, they'll hide under the bed for about a week. Granted, you can still see them because the bed will be two feet off the ground, but you get the picture. Because they are such soft souls they want nothing more than to please their owners, but Thor is an alpha male with a capital *A*.

So when I shouted "*No*," it didn't much matter because he had already crashed through the window.

I climbed in after him as carefully as I could but I still managed to slice my arm on a jagged glass shard.

Derek and Parker were both lying on the carpet, motionless.

My young photographer was closest, so Thor ran to him first, licking his eyes, ears, and nose and flipping up Derek's hand with his giant muzzle.

Parker was lying facedown on the ground, and I ran to him as I reached for my phone.

It wasn't there.

"Shit, I just had it!"

Derek moaned, and Thor and I switched places. He started slobbering all over my boss.

"Derek! Can you hear me? Are you hurt?" I noticed a golf-ball-sized lump on the top of his head.

He groaned, then coughed as Thor nudged Parker.

"Derek, what happened? Come on, talk to me, kid." I patted his arm gently. He twitched.

Behind me, I heard Parker say, "Why am I wet?"

I called Thor back and hustled toward my boss. There was a Crock-Pot on the counter next to the coffee station, napkins, bowls, spoons, and a towel next to it. I grabbed the towel and handed it to Parker as he sat up.

"Why am I on the floor?"

Good question. "What's the last thing you remember?" I asked.

Derek was sitting up too. I went to the sink and wet two paper towels, handed one to each of them.

"I plugged in the slow cooker to heat the chili," Parker said, counting on his fingers. "Derek set the bowls down. We waited a bit, but you were late, so then I was going to head to your office to grab your contact list. I wanted to call your grandmother, let her know Derek would be stopping by."

I asked, "Did you see anything?"

Derek stood up and rubbed his neck. "Nothing. Didn't see anyone, didn't hear anything."

"Someone had to have delivered that lump to your head. Which entrance did you come in?" I asked.

They had both come through the back door.

"Should make sure it's still locked," I said. Someone could have run out after we came through the window.

Parker stood. "No, don't do that. What if someone is still here?"

Another good point. "Right." I felt moistness on my arm. The cut wasn't too deep, but I was bleeding. I reached for a paper towel to mop it up and went to examine Thor.

"Either of you have a phone? I dropped mine coming through the window."

Derek looked at the gaping hole. "Holy shit. You did that? Who do you think you are, Batgirl?"

"Actually, Thor did that." The dog had only minor cuts on the top of his head, thankfully. I hugged him and kissed his nose. He puffed his chest out and sat. "He thinks he's the Incredible Hulk because Lolly dyed him green last Saint Patrick's Day."

Parker said, "That's gonna cost me a fortune." He pulled out a chair, sat, and laid his head on the table.

"Shea, are you okay?"

"Peachy." He did not lift his head. I noticed he didn't have a lump.

Derek reached into his pocket and said, "I got my cell phone."

"Just call Leo, Derek. Don't tie up the 911 system," Parker said.

"Are you serious?" I asked.

"What? It's not life or death," he said.

"But what if there is someone still here?" I asked.

Parker looked at the window. Or rather, the lack thereof. "Pretty sure the Dynamic Duo scared off whoever it was."

He got up and went to assess the damage. I followed.

"Do you need to go the hospital, Parker?" I asked.

"Nah."

"You sure?"

He leaned over and whispered in my ear, "I fainted."

I wrinkled my brow. "What?"

"I saw Derek drop and I fainted."

I whispered back, "Did you see who did it? What he was hit with?"

Behind me, Derek said, "I can't get Leo." He walked over as Parker shook his head at me. "I'll call the station. Try to reach Gus. What are you two looking at?" Derek asked as he dialed.

I looked out the window and just as I was about to say, "Nothing," I saw it.

A white deer.

Ghost of the forest.

She paused, looked right at me, and I felt a bolt of electricity run through my veins. The sun beamed right in my eyes for an instant. Then she was gone.

"Did you see that?" I asked.

"See what?" Parker and Derek both said.

I turned to face them. "That deer. She just ran across the open field."

They hadn't.

When I turned for another glimpse, Ivy was in the truck bed. "Psst!"

I nearly wet myself, she startled me so bad. I held up a finger, signaling her to be quiet for a second.

Derek was saying, "Not sure if anything is missing. We haven't checked it out yet. Thought we'd call you guys first. My camera and my wallet are still with me, though."

Parker excused himself to use the bathroom, and I turned back to the window. "What are you—" I jumped because she was now on the wall and we were nose to nose. "Stop that! What are you doing here?" I hissed.

"I deciphered the code, thought you wanted to know right away. It wasn't easy, I tell you. I think I should get extra credit or like a merit badge or something..."

Ivy was still chattering away when I heard Derek ask Gus, "So what's the story on the stiff they picked up over at the Geraghty house?"

"Shh," I said to Ivy, "I need to hear this."

Derek laughed, "Come on, man. You can't be serious." He paused. I felt Ivy tense. "He didn't just get up and walk away." Derek laughed again and then immediately closed his mouth.

Parker returned, wiping his hands on a brown paper towel.

Derek hung up the phone and stared at it for a couple of beats.

"Well?" I asked. "What did he say?"

Derek looked from me to Parker, back to me.

He put his phone in his pocket. "He said he just got up and walked away."

No one spoke.

Then Ivy whispered, "Whoa. Dude's a zombie."

"There are no such things as zombies," I said.

I made a mental note to confirm that with Birdie later.

I told Ivy to wait for me in the cab of the truck. And to look for my phone.

Derek was talking to Parker. "The body was still on the gurney when the medical examiner got paged. He went to answer it, hit the john, and when he got back, it was gone."

Behind me, Parker said, "Stacy, who are you talking to?"

I turned to face them. "Girl Scout."

Not my finest moment. I would have made a terrible spy because I can't lie to save my life.

"I'll take a box of Thin Mints," Derek said.

Parker said, "Really? I would have pegged you for a Samoa guy."

"No way, man. I hate coconut."

"Guys! She's gone. Forgot her cookies back at the orphanage."

Derek looked confused. Parker just looked disappointed.

"What was she doing at the window?" Derek asked.

"Can we just get back to the runaway corpse, please?" I turned to shut the window because the room grew cold. Except the window was scattered all over the floor in tiny pieces.

I rubbed my shoulders. "Let's go downstairs to my office and wait for the cavalry," I said. "It's freezing in here."

Derek took the lead and flipped every light switch in our path. I tried to steady my mind, my body, searching for a signal. I felt nothing. No nausea, no tingling, no shivers down the spine. I was fairly confident it was only the three of us and Thor inside the newspaper offices. We were halfway downstairs when Parker said, "I'm starving. I'm going to grab the chili."

Just then, something clanked and crashed. Parker grabbed my arm right where the cut was, and I bit my lip to keep from crying out.

We froze in place for a full twenty seconds.

Then Thor trotted out from the conference room, red sauce all over his face.

"Dammit, Thor!" Derek said, "You almost made me crap my drawers."

I was in between Derek and Parker. I glanced from one to the other, said, "Sorry. I forgot to feed him this morning."

"Maybe we can order some sandwiches," Parker said, and we turned to head to my office.

When we got to the door, I remembered I had no key. "Parker, do you have a key to my office? Mine is…at home." Hopefully. Maybe Fiona put everything in the garage. Maybe the attic. I was still kicking myself for rushing off without asking her about it.

Parker fumbled in his coat pocket and I asked Derek what else he knew about Sayer.

"There was mud on the floor around the gurney and a set of footprints trailed out the door. That's all I know. Gus said he'd be right over. Maybe he'll tell us more."

"So he wasn't dead? But he had no pulse. He wasn't breathing," I said as Parker slid the key into the lock.

The buzzer sounded at the front door.

"That's probably Gus. I'll let him in," Derek said and left.

Parker opened the door and flipped the switch.

"What in the world?" he said.

I couldn't see beyond his six-four frame. "What, what is it?"

He stepped aside and I gasped.

"Oh my gods," I whispered.

Chapter 45

IVY GERAGHTY'S PERSONAL BOOK OF SHADOWS
by Ivy Geraghty

Entry #14

While my sister attends to trivial matters, I am planning our attack. I know what steps must be taken now to reclaim our mother and our Birthright! Enemies be Damned! Dark forces are no match for the Geraghty Girls—past, present, or future! I await to join her in the Battle of our lives. Our army will assemble and march on to Victory! (But first I'm totally jonesing for a Cherry Coke and a basket of fries. Off to my Lair.)

—Ivy Geraghty, ~~Junior Apprentice~~ Warrior Goddess (in training)

Chapter 46

My office had been ransacked. Drawers toppled, papers strewn about, pictures ripped off the walls. The destruction was vast, no corner unturned. Luckily my laptop was back at Chance's house, so that was still in one piece, but it would take weeks to organize all the paper files. I couldn't tell what—if anything—was missing. Or what the hell the purpose was, for that matter. What were they were looking for? Or was it just vandalism for the fun of it? Seemed unlikely.

I felt helpless. This was my space, the only space to call my own at the moment. I didn't have my car, didn't have my keys, and my freaking home was being rented without my permission.

My keys! But…the office had been locked. I saw Parker unlock my door.

Whoever did this must have my keys.

"Are you okay?" Parker asked.

The picture of my parents—of me when we were all together, happy—lay on my desk, the frame split. I choked back a sob, closed my eyes, and leaned my head back.

When I opened them, I saw it.

Strung to the ceiling fan, waving around like a streamer, was a doll with red hair, green eyes, and a cape.

Was that supposed to be me? Because if it was, the idiot who constructed it should know I have never kept a cape clean in my life. Plus, I do not wear blue eye shadow.

Helpless? Screw that. That sensation evaporated like steam.

Now I was pissed off.

Quickly, I centered myself, cast a circle of protection. I opened my desk drawer and fished around for my herb sachet to strengthen it. Gone.

I slammed the drawer shut and said, "Parker, would you please get me that salt shaker you keep hidden in your desk?"

"Stacy, you know the doctor said I—"

"Get it!"

He left.

Derek had brought my things to the cottage after the fire, so I didn't have the three-muses sword Birdie had given me as a homecoming present. A letter opener would have to suffice. The Wite-Out was on the floor, so I reached for that and traced a closed pentagram on the desktop. There was still water in the mini fridge, so I grabbed a bottle, uncapped it, and dipped the letter opener inside, imagining white light all around the space. I held it up toward the sky.

The vibrations were strong already.

Or maybe I was shaking because I was so damn angry. I did not have time for black-magic bitches.

Parker snuck in and handed me the salt, and I told him to leave.

When I heard the door click shut, I sprinkled the salt all around the room and then into the water bottle, took a swig, then climbed on top of my desk and chanted.

"Magic of white, surround me with light."

I poured the water all around me, turning a full 360 degrees.

When I closed my eyes, she was there in my head. The white deer. Prophet. Protector. Messenger.

The sign of which meant "Get ready, something is coming."

She was still with me as I continued the spell.

"Magic of black, I thwart this attack!"

My grip was strong on the letter opener as I held it skyward. The lights glared bright, then dimmed. I heard a crackling, and the bulbs on the fan started shaking. I jumped down, took cover under the desk, and one by one the bulbs burst, showering the office with sparks.

When it was over, Parker came in. "You okay, there, kiddo?" Years of working with my father and dinners at the Geraghty house had taught him not to ask too many questions when it came to magic.

I nodded. Felt great, actually. Even the pain in my leg was gone. My shoulder too. I looked down at my arm, hand still gripping the letter opener, and noticed the cut had stopped bleeding. It was healing.

I sighed and picked up the doll from the floor, where it had landed after the light show.

"Is that a voodoo doll?" Parker asked.

Derek and Gus came in at that moment.

"Oh hell, no!" Derek said, backing up. "I got an aunt that's into that shit, freaks me the hell out." He stepped out of the room and said to Gus, "Come on. I am not going in there. I'll show you where they hit us first."

I smiled at that, knowing Parker hadn't actually been struck by anything but had passed out.

The doll was limp in my hand. If it were still charged with any kind of energy, I would have felt it, but there was nothing, just emptiness and not much weight.

There was a note stabbed to the back, puncturing the felt cape through to the body. When I pulled the pin out, red (blood?) oozed from the doll.

The note said in block letters: "Give me what you are hiding or you are next."

Chapter 47

I ran upstairs to find Thor and to see what I could learn about the walking dead from Gus. He was talking to Derek excitedly.

"So, in hand-to-hand combat, Spiderman would beat Batman any day. I mean, first, he's a scientist, right? So he has the smarts, and maybe Batman does too, but he's really just a rich boy with lots of toys. Spidey works alone, has spider sense, the strength, the agility, plus the web shooters."

I cleared my throat.

"Oh, hey there, Stacy. Cinnamon back from Ireland yet?" Gus asked.

Shoot! I forgot about meeting up with my cousin. "Gus, what time is it?"'

He pulled out a phone that looked awfully familiar. "It's one forty-five."

"Is that my phone?" I asked.

He shrugged. "Found it in the parking lot." He handed it over and I saw that I had three missed text messages. All from Monique. I clicked one open.

MUZZLE THIS KID OR I WILL!!!

Not again. Not now!

I ran to the window, and sure enough, the little shit was gone. "Dammit!"

I turned to Gus. "I have to go. Call me if you need anything. But long story short—Derek and Parker were on the ground when I got here and Thor broke the window."

I ducked out, then ducked back in and said, "Oh yeah, I think you caught this earlier, but I'll remind you that someone trashed my office and left a voodoo doll with a note pinned to it threatening my life. You might want to look into that. I left it on the desk."

For a second after I had read the note, I thought about keeping the doll and bringing it to Birdie to glean what she could from it. It's possible I hadn't stripped all its power, but then I decided I would feel much safer with it locked up in an evidence bag at the police station.

The sun was buried behind a sea of clouds as I loaded Thor and hopped into Chance's truck. Images flashed all around my mind like a sideshow. Sayer slumped over the table. Ivy scribbling in her green notebook. The article with the code written in Ogham. Derek and Parker on the floor. The voodoo doll. What was the connection? Did my mother's disappearance have anything to do with Sayer's death? And where was his body? Was it possible that he was still alive? Or had someone stolen his corpse to cover up murder? It wouldn't be the first time.

None of it made any sense. I needed some answers fast. That doll, the note—*give me what you are hiding*—my office trashed because of something I had that didn't belong to me? What could it possibly be? And if that person or persons had the keys to the office, then they had the key to my car and my home.

The cottage. John and Deirdre had a key. But certainly my aunt hadn't given them my key, at least not my entire key ring. Besides, they only knew me through Leo, and John didn't seem like the type to dabble in the dark side of the craft or to marry someone who did. Not that voodoo is all dark magic, but creating a likeness with the intent to threaten or harm the subject is an act of malice.

I wasn't seeing a piece of the puzzle, and that piece was nagging at the back of my mind, tapping on my shoulder, urging me to recognize a clue just out of my grasp. It was too much too fast, and right now I had to collect Ivy, read the decoded message, and get to Birdie's house.

I pulled into a parking spot in front of Down and Dirty, shoving the swirling thoughts to the back of my mind for the moment. I made a point to double-check that the keys were in my pocket as I circled the truck to let Thor out. I wasn't taking any chances, lest more trolls should rear their ugly heads.

Light spilled out from inside the Black Opal across the street, and I wondered if Cin was there inspecting the remodel. Maybe I could pop over after I dragged Ivy out of her favorite watering hole. Goddess only knows why the kid liked to hang out here and what bonded her to Scully, but she wasn't your typical teenager, and I suspected she enjoyed harassing Monique for the sheer delight of watching the woman's eye shadow crack beneath the pressure of a hundred eye rolls. Hell, if I had the time, I'd sit at her bar and harass her all day too.

Thor led the way through the door, and one of the beads from the curtain snagged his collar. He bit at it, jerked his head back, and the whole thing came crashing down on top of him.

He stood there a moment, glanced over his shoulder, then decided the velvet cloak was a good look. He plopped down and sprawled out across the floor. He reminded me of that Carol Burnett skit when she was imitating the famous drapery scene from *Gone with the Wind*.

Monique emerged from the storage room behind the lacquered bar, carrying two bottles of vodka and teetering on four-inch polka-dot slingbacks. The Daisy Duke shorts may have looked great on a woman with curves, but she reminded me of a mannequin in a tween store left in the window too long. "God damn it, Stacy!" She slammed the bottles down and her bleach-blonde pigtail extensions jiggled. I had a sudden urge to yank one out and gag her with it. "Why do you bring that beast into my bar?"

Thor grumbled from his resting spot but he didn't bother getting up.

"Keep your panties on, Monique, if you're wearing any, that is. It can be fixed."

"The whole freaking rod came off!"

I spun around to assess the damage. "The brackets are still there. It's no big deal."

I made a motion for Thor to stand up. He did. The curtain rod slipped off him and I handed it to Monique. "You know, this is probably a fire hazard anyway, having a curtain in the doorway," I said.

"Just fix the damn thing," she snapped.

"Fine, spot me." I climbed on top of a stool and Monique handed me the rod. She held on to the padded seat with her other hand.

The rod cradled onto the brackets easily, but I was still adjusting the curtain tiebacks when Thor decided the chili didn't agree with him and discarded it at Monique's feet. She screamed, jumped back, and the stool I was standing on wobbled, then toppled over. I landed on my back right on top of Thor's vomit.

Holy nutfugget, that hurt. And the putrid smell of the slippery mess wasn't making the situation any more pleasant. However, moving was not an option for a couple of seconds as I caught my wind.

Monique's face twisted into a look of fury she usually reserved for women who stood in the way of her latest conquest. That, and the Mary Kay lady when she ran out of Pole Dancer Red lipstick.

There was a spot of sick the size of a quarter on one of her toes. I really didn't see what the big deal was. There were no customers in the front and the mess could be easily cleaned up.

I struggled to stand up. "I'll clean it up, okay? Calm down."

Her nostrils flared. "Get. Out. Now."

"Monique, just take it easy." Never saw her so angry. "Look, I'm going to grab a towel."

I told Thor to go get Ivy and he trotted into the back room. There was a roll of paper towels behind the bar and I soaked a few, grabbed the whole roll, and went over to clean up the mess.

That was when I saw the penny in the middle of the recycled chili.

I didn't have time to pick it up, though, because behind me, I heard, "Aghhhhh!"

I pivoted to see Monique had a crazed look in her eyes. She came at me, arms flailing in no particular direction.

I'm not usually one to resort to violence. Plus, I promised Cinnamon long ago that if Monique ever needed ass kicking, my cousin could get in the first jab. Since Monique had never tried to steal my husband (mostly because I never had one), I agreed.

So it was quite a relief when I jumped out of the way and Monique skidded across the floor like a drunk monkey on a skateboard and landed face-first in the puke. I hoped that popping sound was just the button on her halter top and not an imploded implant. That was a mess I wasn't about to clean up.

I almost laughed until I heard her wretched sob.

Geez. Could this day get any worse?

As much as that woman made my skin crawl, I couldn't stand to see a fellow human being in pain. She was obviously upset about much more than what had just happened.

I set the towels aside and reached for her hand. "Come on. I'll help you up."

"Get away from me," she sniffled, slapping my hand aside. "You aren't my friend."

"That's probably because you stuck your tongue down my ex-boyfriend's throat five minutes after we broke up." I reached for her again. "Give me your hand."

She peeked at me and I was thankful to see that the muck wasn't on her face, because that very likely would have set off a volcano in my own stomach.

She sighed and grabbed my hand, then wobbled to her feet. I handed her the paper towels.

Her head was still down as she mumbled, "Thanks."

We both cleaned up in uncomfortable silence, and since there wasn't much hope for salvaging my jacket, I tossed it in the trash along with the soiled towels, saving only the penny.

The year held no significance to me. Not my birth year, not Ivy's or anyone else's I could think of at the moment.

I didn't like that one bit, and I suddenly wondered what was taking the dog so long to retrieve Ivy.

Unfortunately, that was the moment Monique decided we were starring in a Lifetime movie. "I don't have any friends," she said softly. "I won't even have customers when your cousin reopens her bar."

I silently cursed the gods for appointing me Counselor of Loose Women.

If Cinnamon could hear what I was about to say, she would kick me. Hard. "Have you ever tried, I don't know… being nice to people?"

Monique narrowed her eyes at me. "I'm nice. I'm just misunderstood."

The only reason I continued was because I was still wiping off dog vomit. "Let's pretend that's true. How about not trying to hump every man you come in contact with? Some women hate that."

She seemed to be considering it for a moment. Her eyebrows wrinkled together like she just ate a lemon, and I guessed that option held no appeal, but I gave her credit for mulling it over. I walked to the trash can and discarded more soiled towels.

Monique risked a smile when I circled back around and for a split second, I was horrified she might hug me. Then the smile fell off her face as she looked past me to the entrance.

"Well, if it isn't the Wicked Bitch of the Midwest," Monique said to Cinnamon.

I squeezed her hand and whispered, "You see, that's what I am talking about. Here's your chance to be nice. Be the bigger person." I nudged her forward and the two women faced each other.

Cinnamon shot me a confused look. Her black hair and dark eyes seemed to deepen a shade as she stared down her nemesis. "And who the fuck are you supposed to be? Trailer Trash Barbie?"

So much for playing nice.

Monique's hands were at her sides, her fists clenched into tiny balls that were growing ever more white by the second. I cleared my throat to encourage her.

In a strained voice she said, "Ha, ha, ha. That's a good one, Cinnamon." Then she looked back at me and I nodded.

Even without the four-inch heels, Monique was a few inches taller than my cousin, but something about Cinnamon's strength and muscular physique seemed to overshadow the blonde bartender.

Cinnamon was trying to grasp just what the hell was happening here. She fumbled with the fray of her ripped jeans and straightened the skull on her beaded T-shirt. "Okay." She glanced around, clearly searching for a hidden camera.

I tapped Monique and she asked in a crackly voice, "Did you have a nice trip?"

Cin looked at her, her left eye twitching ever so slightly, and said, "It was lovely. Thank you for asking."

The two of them stood there, gazing everywhere but at each other.

Finally, after what seemed like hours, while I stood with a lopsided grin because I was hoping against hope that perhaps the days of me getting sucker-punched for stepping between the two of them were over, Monique spoke first.

She shifted her stance toward me. "I tried, Justice, I really did, but I still want to fold her up and stuff her down the garbage chute."

"And I still want to pop one of her implants and watch her fly around the room." Cin turned to Monique and said, "Did she put you up to this?"

Monique said, "Yeah, can you believe it?"

Then they both turned on me and the chattering got so loud, I hardly heard the cries.

"Quiet!" I said. "Do you hear that?"

"Oh, that's just Scully," Cin said. "He's upset about losing some friend. That's why I'm here, actually." She looked from me to Monique. "Do either of you know anyone named Ivy?"

Chapter 48

Monique and I both rushed into the back room. The door was wide open and neither Thor nor Ivy was in sight.

"When did you see her last?" I asked Monique.

"Um, uh…," she stuttered.

I grabbed her shoulders, shook her. "Think!"

"It was when I texted you!"

I fished out my phone, checked the time of the last text message. One thirty. I had left the news office at one forty-five.

I noticed I had two missed calls from Leo and one from Birdie.

Then, a text from Birdie.

Malevolence is all around you. I sense a cataclysmic event. Heed the signs and get to the house as soon as you can. Be smart. Be safe. Be one.

Where had I heard that before?

Monique was still talking. "She was driving me nuts, so I went to organize the storeroom." She bit her lip and looked me in the eye as she said, "Scully was with her, Stacy. I swear, I didn't think it would be a big deal."

Scully wasn't here now, but when had he left? Before I arrived, or had he slipped out the back door while we were still fixing the drapery? Just when that thought passed through my head, a vision pierced my mind, blinded me.

Ivy scribbling in her notebook, red hair covering her face. Backpack on the seat next to her. Right here in this room. Then, more red and then...not a damn thing.

But wait a minute...who would be sending it to me? I only received visions from the dead. Unless...*No.* I refused to consider the possibility.

My eyes swam into focus as I searched for the backpack. Gone. Behind me, Cin was asking who Ivy was.

Her question went unanswered as Monique explained that when she had taken out the trash, Ivy was teasing her about looking like a blow-up doll you might win at a carnival. That was when she ducked into the storeroom.

I ran outside, called for Thor. Looked both ways down the alley. Nothing but Dumpsters, cigarette butts, and stray gum wrappers. It smelled like rotten meat, stale beer—and fear.

Probably radiating off my skin.

I jogged a car length in both directions, but no sign of Ivy.

Then Thor appeared from behind a huge green Dumpster, the lid ajar because someone had overfilled it with a torn-up armchair.

Ivy's backpack dangled from his mouth.

I froze and a sound like a hiccup escaped from Monique.

I raced to where Thor had come from and saw nothing more.

He gently released the backpack into my outstretched hands and my legs could not move fast enough.

I talked as I walked. "You said Scully was out front?" I asked Cinnamon.

She held her questions for the moment. I could only guess she sensed my anxiety. After all, she had Geraghty blood in her veins too, although from her father's side. The gifts are only passed on from mother to daughter, but she had a keen sense of intuition regardless.

"That's where I left him."

The three of us hurried to the front of the building, Thor trailing behind as I rifled through Ivy's bag on the way.

A few bills. Clothes. Her phone. A couple of gemstones. That green notebook she carted everywhere and three pens.

I stopped to unzip the dozen zippers on the damn thing and filtered through them quickly. No article.

No message.

Shit!

Outside, Scully had made his way over to the Black Opal. Two customers approached Down and Dirty, so Monique gave a tiny wave, slapped Thor on the rear to encourage the dog to move out of her path, and turned to head back inside. Before she made it, Thor shook his giant head and tossed a big glob of snot onto her shorts. She hesitated but didn't turn around and the curtain closed on the loogie. Then I noticed the "customers" were the Jehovah's Witnesses from this morning. They waved and I returned the gesture. I almost felt sorry for Monique.

Scully was leaning against the brick, looking up and down the street. He was sipping on a can of Old Style, not bothering to hide it even though open liquor containers are neither legal nor encouraged in Amethyst.

I had never seen Scully show any emotion other than thirst. So when he dabbed his eyes with his sleeves, my heart lurched.

"Come on, Scully. Let's get you inside," I said.

The remodel was spectacular, but I had no time to explore it. I just noticed the sophisticated blue walls, the smart, sturdy circular bar, and the sparkling glass shelves. I told Cinnamon it was beautiful and she smiled.

I wasn't sure if Scully's shriveled hand was shaking because he needed a cocktail or because he was afraid. Cin helped him onto a stool and he had the decency to disapprove, which sent a wave of calm to me.

Scully liked *his* stool, which was still at Monique's place for now. He took a long pull from the beer and sighed. Then, ever so slightly, he reached into his pocket and I held my breath. I felt my cousin's eyes bearing down on me.

It was a piece of paper folded into a tight square. He placed it on the bar top, stared into the mirror behind the bottles.

"Went to take a leak. Found this in the back room after."

He hadn't read it. It was crisp and clean and never unfolded.

But it said, "DO NOT play games with me or the kid gets it," on the outside.

"Scully," I said. "Just lock up when you leave."

"Excuse me?" Cinnamon demanded. "Are you out of your mind?"

I leaned in and said to him, "Don't worry. We'll find her."

To Cinnamon, I said firmly, "Call Tony if you want him to watch the bar, but meet me outside in two minutes." Cinnamon's husband, Tony, owned an auto-repair shop on the edge of town. Since Cinnamon had a thing for muscle cars and musclemen, it was love at first sight.

Inside Chance's truck, with the heater running and Thor sprawled on the back bench, I unfolded the corners of the note.

The book for the girl. Your choice. Will contact for exchange.

In that moment two things occurred to me. One was that in spite of everything the kid had put me through the past few days, I had grown to love Ivy.

The other was that if the kidnapper was referring to the Blessed Book, I didn't have a clue where it was.

Chapter 49

I rummaged through Ivy's backpack again as I waited for Cinnamon. The notebook was on top so I pulled that out and flipped through the pages. The note left by our mother slipped out and I read it again.

And there it was.

Be Smart. Be Safe. Be One. Same as Birdie texted.

What did it mean?

Still, the article she had left for Ivy to discover was nowhere to be found, nor could I find on any of the pages the decoded message. Hopefully, Chance had copied it down.

I texted him to please meet me at the Geraghty Guesthouse.

Cinnamon climbed into the truck then, handed me a cup of coffee, and demanded to know what was going on, so I filled her in on the whole mess as I drove up the hill to the bed-and-breakfast. It was a short trip and she was firing questions at me left and right, which took my focus off the road for just a split second.

Here's a safety tip. If you ever find a voodoo doll with your name on it, while a dead man is roaming the streets and your long-lost sister just got kidnapped by heaven knows who, pass the keys to someone with a steadier hand.

She just appeared in the middle of the road and I swerved to avoid her, promptly smashing Chance's truck into a tree.

My body jerked forward and hot coffee splattered across my turtleneck. Then we came to an abrupt halt. I wasn't driving that fast, thankfully. Cin and I looked each other over and then I unhooked my seat belt to check on Thor. Everyone seemed to be okay.

Cinnamon looked at me like a snake had just crawled out of my head.

"What was that?" she said.

"I didn't want to hit her." Crap. Chance was going to kill me. He loved this truck. Maybe he wouldn't notice.

"Who?"

"The white deer. Didn't you see her?" I peered across the woods, but she must have fled.

Cin said she hadn't seen a thing. We were only a couple blocks from the house, so we all climbed out and started walking. I finished telling Cinnamon the rest of the story.

She had a funny look on her face when she asked, "So Parker didn't actually get hit?"

I wrinkled my brow. "That's your question? I just revealed that you may have another cousin, and one of Birdie's guests took a header into the kitchen table, and *that's* the question you have?"

"Oh, I have more, but hear me out. Parker didn't get clocked. He said he fainted. That's odd enough, but then he also had a key to your office."

"He has a key to every office." I looked at her. "You don't think…" I shook my head. "No, no way. Why would he trash my office? And how could he have hit Derek without Derek knowing it?"

"Brings me to point two. Didn't Derek say once he had an aunt who practiced voodoo? Remember, when we were visiting that kid in the hospital to find out about the fire?"

He had said that then, and he had just reiterated it to me an hour ago. This I told Cin.

I stopped walking, and Thor took the opportunity to scratch his neck. His tiger's eye was still in my pocket, so nothing jingled beneath the force of his huge paw. I took it out, put the third penny inside the locket, and went to clip it onto his collar.

Just then, pictures of the white deer flashed in my mind, rapidly, alternating between images of a woman who looked a lot like Fiona but with longer hair and a gauzy white gown not of this time. I had to bend over to steady my body. Only then did Maegan speak, her voice a soft symphony in my ears.

There are three only whose calling is a benefit to their people: the Warrior on the field of battle, the Guardian of sacred truth, and the Seeker of Justice, wherever she may be.

The voice faded and I stood.

Cin was looking at me with concern, and Thor trotted over and stood next to me. I placed my hand on his back for balance.

That seemed important, so I took out Ivy's notebook, flipped to the last page, and jotted down, "Guardian, Warrior." I had a pretty good idea who the Seeker of Justice was.

Then a wind grabbed the pages, flipping them backward until the notebook rested on Ivy's last entry.

I couldn't believe what I was seeing. "Son of a sockcucker," I said.

"What is it?" Cinnamon asked.

"Apparently there is a Warrior among us," I told her, glancing over Ivy's signature.

So then who was the Guardian?

Cin and I kept hashing out the events that had transpired in her absence, and I was grateful, finally, to have someone to talk to about it. I wasn't especially looking forward to spilling my guts to Birdie, but it had to be done. I wasn't about to screw around with the wack job who had apparently killed a guy in my grandmother's kitchen, left me a voodoo doll with a cryptic message, and then hijacked my sister. Enough was enough. He or she would get the damn book if it was so important. Surely I would get another message instructing me on where to make the exchange.

Afterward, maybe I could find my mother. *Our* mother.

Then a thought occurred to me. Was she the Guardian? And if so—what was she guarding?

Chapter 50

I was thinking about the questions I still had for Birdie as we rounded the corner. Rushing out to the police station, when she could have easily waited for the cops to come to the house? That one still had me scratching my head. Then just taking off and leaving me there. Why?

Actually, that was probably some form of punishment, I was certain. She must have known I had lied, must have sensed I had never left town, but did she know why? Did she know about Ivy?

I spotted Leo's cruiser in the driveway. No other cars, thank Goddess. The guests were probably running around town, tracking down clues for that murder-mystery event this evening. Boy, was I glad I hadn't gotten roped into helping with that, seeing as how I had my own unsolved mysteries to contend with.

I took the steps slowly in a vain attempt to postpone the inevitable. The air was stagnant this afternoon. Not chilly anymore, no scent of blossoms or herbs, just damp earth.

I took a deep breath and twisted the handle, but the door was locked.

Just what I needed.

I cranked the old-fashioned bell and pressed the doorbell that chimed in the private quarters, just to be safe.

We stood there a few seconds, waiting for someone to answer, and I suddenly felt bad that Cinnamon had come home to this situation. "I hope you took lots of pictures. I want to hear all about your trip when…you know," I said.

She just rolled her eyes.

Then I realized the locket was still in my hand. I clipped the tiger's eye back on Thor's collar.

A moment later, Fiona answered the door and I whispered a small thank-you to the gods that it wasn't Lolly.

She wore a smart black suit and a stern look on her face. Thor hopped and wiggled all around her, kissing her hand.

"That's a good boy," she said, scratching his ear. She handed him a giant bone. "You've done well. Go lie down for a while."

That reminded me. Hadn't I heard Chance mention something about a cat as I left his house?

"Fiona, have you seen Moonlight? Not to mention all my stuff?"

Her face was stone as she said, "Moonlight had another calling."

That was all she said, and it made me shiver. I didn't ask what she meant by "another calling."

Cinnamon and I exchanged an uneasy glance and my stomach didn't just have butterflies. There were sparrows flying around inside, dive-bombing a worm farm.

Fiona spun on one foot and walked straight ahead. We followed.

Nervous did not even cover how my body felt on that long walk down the corridor. I sensed Cin felt it too. Like tiny ants crawling all over my skin. Something was happening. Something—not good.

The house was quiet. I saw no guests anywhere, and I wondered if they had checked out with all the commotion. Or had been forced to find other accommodations.

Just as we approached the kitchen, I smelled the faint scent of an herb I could not identify. Hemlock? Hell, I hoped not. Hemlock is very powerful but extremely dangerous.

Lolly was at the apothecary table, dipping a gloved hand into a steaming bowl of liquid. On the table before her, laid out in shiny variations of length, cut, and adornment, were a collection of ritual blades. She was dipping one hand into the potion and holding a sword with the other as she swiped the concoction across it in swift strokes.

"What is she doing?" Cinnamon whispered.

Lolly didn't look up, just kept working. "Empowering the blades for ritual. My guess is hemlock, that's the strongest herb to charge a tool."

Fiona opened the door that led upstairs to their private quarters. She turned, swept her arm out, and said, "After you."

I shoved Cinnamon forward and said, "You first."

She whirled around, pushed me back, and said, "Hell no. You're the freaking Seeker. Besides, I didn't do anything to piss them off."

"Fine." What's the worst that could happen? "It's not like they're going to kill us." I chuckled.

Behind me, Lolly sharpened two blades together. I heard Cinnamon suck in some air.

The stairs were dark and Fiona hadn't bothered to turn on the light as we walked up them. I was growing irritated with all this cloak-and-dagger stuff. Ivy was missing. I didn't know who had her, and nothing else really mattered until I got her back.

I picked up the pace and turned right at the top of the stairs.

"Wrong way, dear," Fiona said.

I faced her. "What are you talking about? There's nothing but a wall there."

Cinnamon stood silent.

Fiona walked over to the wall and waved her hand across the eight-foot gilded oil painting of Danu, mother of Celtic gods, sitting in a golden chair with lion's-head feet, a gleaming chalice in her hand. There was a ruby on the chalice and Fiona pressed it. When she did, I swear Danu looked at me with disapproval.

To my complete astonishment, the painting shook loudly, then swung open to reveal a secret passageway.

My mouth must have been hanging on the floor. I had grown up in this house, but never had I seen this hidden room. I stepped inside, not really thinking it through first, because the sheer curiosity of the whole thing propelled me forward.

When I got to the end of the dark narrow hall, I hit a brick wall.

"Uh, Fiona. I don't see which way I'm supposed to go here."

"Forward, of course," she said.

I felt around. "Nope. There's no opening. No doorway."

Cinnamon muttered something about a fun house and how she always got roped into my drama. I ignored her.

Fiona said. "Close your eyes, Stacy. Close your eyes and open your mind. Just because you cannot see a thing doesn't mean it isn't there."

That was the dumbest thing I had ever heard. "Actually, that's exactly what that means."

"Really?" Her voice was laced with sarcasm. "Tell me then, can you see the air that surrounds you?"

"No, of course not, but—"

"But you know it exists, isn't that true?"

It wasn't exactly the same thing, but arguing would be wasted effort. "Point made, Fiona."

"Now then, close your eyes and imagine a doorway."

I heard her say something about all those years at college and for what...then I took a deep breath and did as she instructed.

When I opened my eyes, there was a small doorway, framed in ornate gilded gold. Just like the frame around the painting, actually.

We had to duck down to crawl through, and Cin said, "You couldn't have imagined it bigger?"

I stopped short when we made it to the other side and her head rammed into my ass.

"Dude, not cool," Cin said.

Panic rose within me as I rose to my feet.

No! I couldn't possibly be seeing this.

"Birdie! What have you done?" I asked.

Chapter 51

Birdie was wearing a black ritual cape, her makeup more colorful than usual. Hanging from her neck was the largest silver pentagram I had ever seen. Each point was adorned with pyrite and different variations of obsidian. Both are used to defeat dark magic and can shield—even reverse—the energy of a psychic attack.

Her appearance was not what had me on tilt, however.

In the center of the room was a massive round table, intricately carved with Celtic symbols and battle scenes, with beautiful ships and towering cliffs, highlighted with gold filigree. There were thirteen chairs—all red velvet, all as beautifully crafted as the table.

It looked like King Arthur's round table. And for all I knew, it could have been. But before I could ask if she was indeed the keeper of the Holy Grail, I had a more pressing subject to address.

Mainly, the two men slumped in chairs opposite each other.

Chance and Leo. Each with a tiny voodoo doll in front of him.

I would have thrown up, but I hadn't eaten all day.

A quick scan of the room told me Sayer wasn't here, at least. Little comfort, but I guess two bodies were better than three.

"Take off your shirt, Anastasia."

"Pardon me?"

She smiled at me with her lips, but her eyes were fierce. "It is time to remove your stitches."

She produced a blade with a sharp hook at the end, and Cinnamon squeaked from somewhere behind me. I backed way up. Into Fiona. Who pushed me forward. Then Lolly came in looking like Indiana Jones meets Edward Scissorhands. A long black duster jacket hardly hid the knives secured to her waist, and the hat could have come directly from Harrison Ford's costume department.

I knocked Cinnamon into a chair as I scrambled to get away from them.

"Sit down, child. What is wrong with you?" Fiona asked.

This was it. I had lied to Birdie about everything and she was going to have Lolly fillet me right here in this private torture chamber, and no one would ever know.

I closed my eyes and told Cin I loved her.

No response.

I opened one eye and saw my cousin facedown on the table.

"Cin!" Oh geez, they got to her already. But how? "She didn't do anything! You can't kill her too!"

Birdie rolled her eyes, and Fiona and she exchanged a glance. "Oh, for the love of Rhiannon. We didn't kill Cinnamon. Why are you being so dramatic?"

I scuffled over and poked Cinnamon.

She stirred. "What? Sorry, did I doze off?" Her words slurred. "Must be the jet lag. And that last Xanax I popped at the bar. Making me be nice to Monique...oh, almost forgot. Here, Birdie." She pulled a postcard from her pocket and handed it to our grandmother. Then her head smacked the table and she started snoring.

I heaved a huge sigh of relief.

"Can we please remove your stitches now? Because we have lots to talk about, young lady." Birdie did not allow me to answer her. She just pulled out a chair, told me to sit, and yanked the sleeve up my arm.

She frowned when she examined the spot where the bullet had grazed my shoulder. "They're gone. Did you remove them yourself?"

The spell in my office. Somehow it had lent a healing energy to my body. I didn't want to lie (again), so I said, "In a way." I stood. "But look, first things first. What is going on here?"

Lolly busied herself laying a velvet cloth across the table, placing the knives on top of it, while Birdie explained that Chance had arrived first. Loyal as he was to me, he was no match for the three of them or their skills. Eventually, despite insisting that he only wanted to wait for me so he could pick up his truck (glad I didn't have to face that at the moment), he spilled his guts about Ivy and the note from my mother, and he gave Birdie the message we had decoded.

I perked up at that. "You have it? Oh, thank Brighid. Birdie, I wanted to tell you, I did, but I wasn't sure what to believe or even if Ivy was related to us. I swear I was going to come to you, but then the thing with Sayer happened and—"

She interrupted. "Which leads me to your friend Leo's arrival."

I looked at Leo. His mouth hung open, head drooped back, and I felt a pang of guilt. If it weren't for me, he wouldn't be in this situation. Whatever it was.

"He told me about Mr. Sayer not being present in the morgue. Said there was video of him leaving." She leaned forward. "Do you have any idea what that means?"

"It means you didn't stab him?"

She frowned at that. "No, but perhaps I should have. I'm not sure it was an accident that he was in the Honeycuts' suite. Or later, in the kitchen, for that matter."

I recalled Mrs. Honeycut's claim that Birdie had been outside last night, holding a dagger.

The knives on the table gleamed, and I wondered if I had the guts to pull a Juliet because I was pretty sure I did not want to hear any more, nor did I want to go to prison for being an accessory after the fact.

Chance and Leo were still.

Birdie continued. "There is a powerful substance called tetrodotoxin, derived from the puffer fish."

Lolly blew air into her cheeks, held her breath, and blinked at me. Then she pulled a lipstick from her pocket and smeared it all around her mouth, smacking her gums together. She must have forgot to put her teeth in. She started arranging the knives like stick people.

"In Japan, the puffer fish is considered a delicacy, if prepared properly," Fiona said.

"And if it isn't?"

"It can be deadly," Birdie said.

"So what does this have to do with Sayer?"

Birdie walked around the table, touching Chance, then Leo, on the shoulder. Neither moved, and I felt a lump in my throat.

"There is a way to use the substance that will allow for the victim to show all the signs of being deceased—breathing so shallow it isn't detected, paralysis of the limbs, pulse rate slowed to a trickle. But the victim can survive and revive if given a small amount."

"And you think this is what happened? Why would anyone want to do that? What purpose would it serve?" I asked.

Fiona said, "In Haiti tetrodotoxin has been used to control people, to enslave them, or to coerce them to do another's bidding. It's called zombie powder."

Oh, you have got to be kidding me. I walked around to Lolly, filtered through her duster jacket, and pulled out a bottle of vodka. It stung going down my throat, but since my ears were burning at what I had just heard, I figured it was a wash.

"Zombie powder," I said, capping the bottle. I handed it to Lolly, who also took a hit. "You really expect me to swallow that?"

"Look it up on the Giggle if you like, dear. It's very common in voodoo practices as well. Serves as a punishment for a crime," Fiona said.

"First of all, Fiona, it's Google, not Giggle. Second, why would anyone use it on a guest at your inn?"

"To kill in a way that would never be detected by the authorities. Not many in this country would check for the poison unless the deceased had taken a trip to the island."

Or if he knew someone who practiced. Like Derek's aunt.

I shivered. "So." I nodded toward the men in my life. "Are they zombies too?" The words felt like chalk in my mouth, and I wished Ivy were here.

Birdie snapped her head as if she had been slapped. "Of course not! We abide by Celtic law in this house! And we do not dabble in darkness."

"Then what's with the voodoo dolls, and why aren't the two of them moving?" I asked.

"Honestly, Anastasia, it's like you pick and choose which lessons to retain from your teachings." She walked over to Chance and picked up the doll in front of him. "This is a protection poppet, filled with nettle, angelica, and purple sage. As I told you in my message, there is malevolence surrounding us, the house, perhaps the entire town. It is strong. I felt it last night, which is why I took great precautions to protect what is mine and ours. And how do you fight magic?"

"With magic," I said. "Is that why you were outside holding the dagger? To perform a ritual?"

Birdie nodded.

"And rushing off to the police station while a dead body, er, zombie"—*did I really just say that?*—"was in your kitchen? Why did you do that?"

"I didn't know what had happened to Mr. Sayer at the time, but as soon as John asked you to call the police chief, I felt the vibration. It was a warning that somehow Leo or his place of work would be engulfed in the venom that approaches. So I went there under the guise of assisting the investigation to bespell the station house and all who enter."

The voodoo doll. I'd left that for Gus to bag as evidence. Perhaps that would have sent an evil energy to the place. I relayed the scene at the newspaper offices to them quickly.

Birdie nodded as if she expected as much.

Fiona said, "We also needed this." She pulled something shiny from her pocket.

It was Gus's badge. "Why on earth—"

"For your anointment," Fiona said. "We needed a symbol of justice. We'll return it, of course."

Of course. "My anointment?" I repeated.

The three of them bobbed their heads.

I sighed and pulled out a seat next to Cinnamon, who was still managing to sleep through this little trip into the Twilight Zone. I made a mental note to borrow a Xanax when this was all over.

"Okay, let's just put that on the back burner for now, shall we? What are they doing here?" I pointed to Chance and Leo.

"Lolly's special tea, Stacy," Fiona said. "They're only sleeping now so that we could charge the poppets and direct the protective energy to them."

Birdie said, "I hardly think they would have cooperated otherwise."

"They'll be waking soon. Couldn't have them walking around as targets, especially with how protective the two of them can be when it comes to your welfare," Fiona said. Then she looked at me sternly. "And Danu only knows the kind of trouble you can get yourself into."

Right. Like it was all my fault some voodoo warlock is running around poisoning people with fish guts and hanging troll dolls from the rafters.

"Well, that's good news, because someone will certainly notice if the chief of police is missing, and since his car is parked out front, I'd say it's a good bet they'd beeline it over here."

"It's your fault, you know," Birdie said.

Oh, come on! I looked up and they were all three staring me down, arms folded over.

"My fault? How the hell is this"—I waved my arm across the table—"*my* fault?"

"You know we don't believe in hell, so stop using that word in our presence," Birdie said.

"Fine. How in fucked-up fairyland is this my fault?"

Harsh, I know, but I was blazing mad now.

Birdie began organizing the knives according to length and was notably silent for several moments. "You should have come to us the minute that girl set foot on your doorstep. We would have taken action far differently."

Fiona pulled a green cape from a wardrobe closet. "We would not have had to scramble to cast protection spells, resort to stealing, or had to lure these poor dears up here."

I didn't even want to know how they did that.

"What does she have to do with any of this?" I asked.

Fiona raised an eyebrow at Birdie, who produced a slip of yellow notebook paper. For some reason, that gesture made me think of Ivy's backpack, still wrapped around me. It seemed heavier just then.

"Did you not decode this message?" she asked.

"I did, but I didn't string the words together. What does it say?"

Fiona leaned in and asked, "You still don't know?"

"Know what?" I asked.

Lolly smacked her head and took another shot from the bottle. Fiona told her to make sure that the men would be sleeping a bit longer. Lolly fumbled through her coat, pulled out a small brown vial, raised Chance's eyelid, then

Leo's, and dropped liquid into each one. Then Fiona helped Cin, grumbling in a Xanax-induced haze, to her feet and carted her off.

Birdie explained that the guests had all been rehoused to other inns and hotels, so Cin could rest comfortably in a bed. Fortunately, she explained, the guests thought it was all part of the murder-mystery weekend.

A thought flickered through my mind, and I recalled I had never met the guests booked into the third room of the main house.

Birdie towered over me and said, "Anastasia. I have a story to tell you."

Chapter 52

A perfection of means, and confusion of aims, seems to be our main problem.
—Albert Einstein

She began with the Book of Ballymote, since I had proven that the story was instilled in me through decoding the message written in Ogham. Decoding the letters wasn't tough, but with the words circled within the article, I really wasn't able to formulate entire sentences in my head.

"What you may not know is that the first page of the text has been missing, purposefully so, for nearly five hundred years."

"What do you mean, purposefully so?" I asked.

Lolly was seated next to an unconscious Chance, and Fiona joined her. They were busy mixing oils together, and every so often they would measure me.

"Patience, Anastasia," Birdie said. "You seem knowledgeable about the history of the book. So you must recall that the original manuscript had been stolen and recovered repeatedly."

I nodded.

"The reason for that is it once revealed treasured information."

Well, duh.

"Before I continue, I must ask what you know about Ivy."

I hadn't told her yet about the note Scully had given me, and that Ivy was seemingly missing. For the moment, I needed to learn everything Birdie wanted to share with me, and I needed to make sure that Ivy wasn't a threat to us—inadvertently or otherwise.

I reached around for the backpack and pulled the zipper open. I dug inside for Ivy's notebook and slipped out the page our mother had scribbled on, slid it to Birdie. Lolly skated some reading glasses across the table to my grandmother and she put them on.

Birdie scanned the note, then flipped through Ivy's journal, motioning for her sisters to flank her. They read in silence and I was wondering what any of it meant.

Finally, Birdie spoke. "Okay then. I think this is all the proof we need to send to the council for confirmation. Anoint her."

Lolly and Fiona nodded, and before I could protest, each took to tossing oil on me, rubbing crystals through my aura, beating my back with herbal brooms, and fitting me with a multi-sheath belt. You know, your typical anointment process.

I said, "The council?"

Birdie sighed and produced the postcard from her pocket. "I asked Cinnamon to do me a little favor while she was in Ireland. This is what she brought back."

The photograph on the front was of a castle. The back said only, "It is time."

Then I thought of the white deer. Prophet. Protector. *Get ready.*

I explained to Birdie the sightings and how I felt it was Maegan speaking to me.

She smiled, slapped the table, and said, "Very good. You recognized the message. Now recognize the danger. People will—and have—killed for the information I am about to tell you."

Lolly grinned at me, a gaping space where her teeth should have been, and Fiona winked. Fiona grabbed a makeup kit. Lolly went to the wardrobe.

She fumbled through the garments quicker than I had ever seen her move. She didn't bother looking back as she tossed out a black leather jacket, matching chaps, black boots with three-inch heels, a bustier that I could never make proud, and what every girl wants her seventy-plus aunt to pull out of a box—studded wristbands.

Yay me.

I didn't share their enthusiasm or their fashion sense, but I humored them to get through this conversation. "So who is the message from? What is it time for? And who are the council?"

Birdie stood, took a deep breath, and said as if rehearsed, "There are three only whose calling is a benefit to their people: the Warrior on the field of battle, the Guardian of sacred truth, and the Seeker of Justice, wherever she may be." She looked at me and said, "The council is a select group sworn to uphold Celtic law. They confirm these three of every generation. It has already been confirmed that you are the Seeker. I suspect Ivy is the Warrior. And the time has come for your calling."

My aunts nodded in agreement.

"And the Guardian?" I asked.

Birdie frowned. "I don't know yet, but whoever it is, is close." She looked at Chance, then Leo.

"Oh, please don't drag them into it," I said.

Birdie paced. "It's only a hunch, but I feel it is someone near. Someone in town this very day." She turned to stare at me. "Someone who has come in contact with the Warrior."

Well, that's just shiny and perfect. That kid had run off to Down and Dirty so many times it could be any number of barflies. It could be those Jehovah's Witnesses. Hell, it could even be Monique. And wouldn't that just serve her right?

And then it made sense. *Be Smart. Be Safe. Be One.* Or at least as much sense as any of this could make. She must have been referring to the Seeker, the Warrior, the Guardian.

I stood, crossed to Birdie. "What about my mother? Couldn't she be the Guardian if we are from the same family? Doesn't this mean that she's Ivy's mother? That Ivy is my sister?"

She looked at me with a flash of sorrow. "The three are rarely from the same clan."

"Well, then what does all this mean? How would she possibly know about us? The Geraghtys? The note says..." I fumbled for it, read it aloud. "'Always believe in yourself and the clan of the Geraghtys.'"

Birdie said, "I see that. But read it again. See the words that are there, not what you wish them to be."

I read the note again as if for the first time. Flipped through the pages of the notebook. I saw then what Birdie was pointing out to me.

There was simply no confirmation either way. It didn't say trust in *our* clan. Ivy's notes never said the woman who raised her told her she *was* my sister. But she believed that. And I wanted to as well.

"Then tell me, Birdie, what is the connection?"

"I already did. You are the Seeker, she the Warrior."

I shouted, "Of what?"

She explained that the three original three scribes of the Ballymote writings had sworn a blood oath directly onto the first page of the document to protect its most valuable secret. The writers appointed a Guardian to ward over the manuscript, a Warrior to combat enemies and thieves, and a Seeker to bring to justice those who broke their vows or the law.

"Most generations," Birdie said, "there is only one from each clan. Occasionally, it was possible there were two members from a single clan. Mostly due to the betrayal of an original three."

By the tone of her voice, I guessed the punishment for betrayal was a long walk down a short pier.

"Birdie, I know the authors of that text and not one was named Geraghty."

She gave me a wicked smile. "Do you think your ancestors are stupid enough to keep their original names so that all the world could track down the descendants?"

Fiona paused from playing makeup artist. "Especially with the Internook."

"Internet, Fiona," I said.

"What's the difference?" she asked.

"Never mind."

Birdie sat down and so did I. "The clans of O'Duignan, O'Droma, and McSheedy are presently Geraghty, Delaney, and Mahoney."

Mahoney—why did that name ring a bell?

"Okay, so we are tasked with guarding the first page from the ancient Ballymote book. So where is it?"

"It's best I don't tell you right now," Birdie said.

"What if I refuse?"

Lolly slapped the wristbands on me and began stuffing knives in the belt.

Birdie said, "Not an option."

Lolly pretended to slice across her throat with a dagger.

"Well, how am I supposed to protect it?"

"You'll find the Guardian."

"And how do I do that?"

Fiona piped up, "Guardians all have one thing in common, dear. They all have a birthmark in the shape of the trinity on their backsides."

This was too much. "So I'm just supposed to approach random strangers and ask them to drop their drawers?"

"Don't be silly," Fiona said, and strapped on the chaps. Then she yanked my own shoes off and secured me into the boots that would likely ruin my chances of escaping a homicidal maniac.

Birdie said, "Look, you have found the Warrior, so all you need to do is find the Guardian and the secret will be safe from whomever threatens it as soon as you are united."

"Can you at least tell me the big secret?"

Because I swear to Christ if it's the recipe for potato pancakes or something, I'll burn the page myself.

"In time."

Which brought me to Final Jeopardy. Or so I thought. "What if, let's say—hypothetically, of course—I don't know exactly where the Warrior is? What happens then?"

Birdie was contemplating the question, gauging to see if I was serious, so I decided to hand over the note that Scully had found.

"So then it's true. It's time," Fiona said, reading over Birdie's shoulder.

"You keep mentioning that. Time for what?" I asked.

Birdie folded the note and stuffed it in her pocket.

"Every hundred years or so, when faith is weakened…" She looked at me as if I were personally responsible for all the debauchery on the planet. "The Hunters come."

"The Hunters. Okay, who are the Hunters?"

Fiona said, "Sometimes it can be a rogue member of an original clan, but more often than not they are outsiders. The fact that it looks like someone tried to eliminate Mr. Sayer may indicate there are two of them."

"Hunters can be historians, scholars, archaeologists— people who have learned the legend of Ballymote and want to discover it for themselves," Birdie said.

"Or, rather, steal the secret for themselves," Fiona said.

"The secret you can't tell me about," I said.

She nodded.

"That's on the page you can't tell me the location of."

Birdie and Fiona exchanged a glance.

Frodo never had to go through this.

"She must know now," Fiona said. "The note changes everything. There may be a rogue. Which would be far more dangerous than a dabbler." She tossed some glitter on Gus's badge, blew it in my face, and rubbed the badge over my heart.

Birdie took a deep breath. "The original page was destroyed before the book was copied in 1887. There was concern that too many copies would jeopardize the mission of protecting the sacred text. And so"—Birdie paused, looked at me—"It was agreed that each of the three clans would begin their own stories, their own...books. Within the manuscripts, the matriarch was tasked to find a way to embed precisely one-third of what was on that long-ago-destroyed page. So that way, the three that are most important to our people—the Seeker, the Guardian, the Warrior—are all needed in order to properly piece the information together. It was a way to provide checks and balances. You see, all three would be needed to compile the information."

"The Blessed Book," I whispered.

"Yes," Birdie said.

But I needed the book to get Ivy back. What other choice was there?

"Birdie, the note Scully found said we could trade the book for Ivy. I cannot risk her life over this."

"We risk many lives if the Blessed Book finds its way into enemy hands. It is not an option," she said.

Lolly said, "I think the boys are stirring."

"What do you mean, we risk many lives? Like as in war? What's the goddamn secret?" I asked.

Birdie stood tall and said, "I have told you enough. Find the Guardian."

She glanced back, and to wipe that smug look off her face I said, "If the birthmark is what identifies the

Guardian, I can tell you it isn't either of them." I grinned at her.

She scowled.

Fiona said, "She's ready." Then she sprayed patchouli all over me. I freaking hate patchouli.

Lolly turned me to face a full-length mirror.

The person staring back was not me. She was a vampire slayer with a day job as a hooker. I took one long, pathetic breath and said, "Where do I start?"

Birdie came behind me, draped the pentagram necklace over my head, and said, "Darkness is drowned by three lights: nature, knowledge, and truth. Start there."

Once she started talking like Yoda, there was no reasoning with her.

Chapter 53

My grandmother shoved a piece of notebook paper in my hand, gave a last warning of impending doom, and slammed the door in my face.

Fine by me. I did not want to be there when her prisoners awoke, for two reasons. One—and most importantly—I didn't want Chance or Leo to see me dressed like a reject from a *Twilight* movie casting call. Two, I was betting they might have a few questions as to what had happened to the last hour and a half of their lives, and since we've already covered that I'm a horrible liar, I wanted to get the muck out of there.

I held the note tight in my hand as I rushed down the hallway. The door to the last room was open, so I stuck my head in and saw Cinnamon sleeping soundly. I decided not to wake her as I headed for the kitchen. There was a lot to do, but even a Seeker of Justice guarding an ancient Secret History of the World, or whatever the heck it was, needed fuel.

The kitchen was a lot quieter than this morning, and I didn't see any police no crossing tape, so I headed straight for the fridge and poked around until the counter was covered with all the makings of a sandwich. Since I hadn't eaten all day and because I was dressed like Elvira's less endowed sister, I decided I had earned the right to eat real bacon. On top of real mayonnaise—no Miracle Whip, thank you. Why do they even make that stuff?

The stillness of the room, the soft hum of the refrigerator, and the smoky scent of a processed pork product helped to clear my mind. I sat down at the table with a tall glass of milk, a pad of paper, and the best honkin' BLT this side of the Mississippi.

I unfolded the Ogham translation and laid it in front of me.

The time of The Hunters has come. I had hoped Ivy would be older for this battle, but she has been trained well. Protecting her has been an honor and a privilege, but the child no longer belongs to me. She belongs to the world. Ivy, your loyalty now aligns with the council. Stacy, I know you will serve her well. Your confirmation came at such a young age that I have no doubt the two of you and your combined talents will serve and protect the treasure at all costs. Remember, the three highest causes of the true human are: Truth, Honor, and Duty.

The only clue I have uncovered as to where the attack will happen is this: The river is clear on this fateful night, though the Hunters are hidden well within sight.

Be Smart. Be Safe. Be One.

P.S. Sewn into the lining of Ivy's backpack is a little token of insurance.

I tore through the bag, pulling out stitches and ripping into zippers.

Finally, I found it. It was a key to a safe-deposit box. Taped to the back was the address of a bank branch about forty minutes away.

"*Mom worked at a bank for a while.*" Ivy's words echoed in my ear. That was when I had asked her what was glowing in her backpack. She thought it was from the anti-counterfeit pen, but it was really the black-light ink.

Wait a second. That pen. Ivy told me that Mom talked about phony money on the telephone.

Phony money. Were Ivy's young ears not hearing properly? Could she really have been saying Mahoney money?

Geraghty, Delaney, Mahoney. I jotted the names on the pad of paper and started listing out what needed to be done to protect a treasure I knew nothing about. No easy task, but I guess knowledge and truth, as Birdie said, might help. Not sure how nature would play into it, but you choose the best tools for the job and go from there.

First on tap was calling in the crash and getting the truck towed back to Chance's place. Then I had to grab the guest book and receipts. Hopefully, Birdie knew where everyone had rebooked so I could drop in and speak to them after I went to the bank. If it was someone in this house who had assaulted Sayer (I still wasn't completely convinced on the whole walking-dead theory), then that person must be a Hunter. Maybe. Or he or she could be the Guardian and have discovered Sayer to be a Hunter. Either way, if all this were true, then it should somehow lead me to Ivy. Since the last names I knew so far were Sayer and Honeycut, my guess was that the third party might have had the name of Delaney or Mahoney.

My head was pounding, so I went to the medicine cabinet in search of relief. Two aspirins later, it hit me that I still didn't know where all my crap was, so I texted Birdie, who wrote back that it was in the shed.

Hmm. Maybe that was where she'd hidden the book.

I still had two missed calls from Leo, so I hit voice mail and listened to him explain he was coming to the house to tell us something, asking me to meet him. I was pretty sure it was about Sayer's missing body. I deleted it, and the next message was tenser, his voice concerned about my office break-in. "Please just call me and tell me you're okay."

I washed my hands with lavender soap, and when I looked back in the mirror I saw something far more frightening than my own reflection.

A woman. Gagged and tied to a bed.

I couldn't see her face, but the hair—the hair was unmistakable.

Ruby red.

I yelped, spilling the aspirin bottle over, and the tiny pills ran down the drain, chasing the running water.

I shut the water off, closed my eyes, and called to Maegan. She had to be the one sending me the visions.

"Mother of my mother's mother, please, unveil the message you're sending me. Is the woman a Geraghty? Is she my mother?"

This time Maegan came in the form of a white tiger with piercing green eyes. It was a beautiful creature, standing regally in a meadow. I watched in awe as the scene turned from day to night. The tiger crossed the tall grass and lay down with determination. Suddenly, she charged a group of gazelle and pounced on one, dragging her prey off into the woods.

I stood there horrified and feeling sorry for the gazelle. But then three cubs came scampering out from behind a log and happily tore into their dinner. I watched them eat for a second or two until the mother's eyes narrowed. Her ears flickered and perked, and her movement halted.

Then, behind her, a Bengal tiger approached.

"Look out!" I said.

She whirled and faced the intruder. The two tigers stood, heads lowered, studying each other and snarling for several moments. The white one carefully placed herself between her cubs and the intruder.

The Bengal charged without warning and the white tiger lunged for its throat. Huge teeth flashed and snapped and in a fit of fury, the two ripped at each other's bodies. Bits of fur and blood splattered across the landscape like gunfire, and I cried out, "No!"

The scene fizzled out instantly, without revealing the victor.

"Wait! What happened?"

"Who are you talking to and why are you dressed like Catwoman?"

I whirled to see Leo standing behind me.

"Don't get me wrong"—his eyes strolled up and down my body—"I love the boots. This is just a new look for you."

I brushed past him and Chance came around the corner.

Geez, they couldn't keep them up there for five more minutes?

"Hey, where's my truck?" Chance said.

Damn. I didn't want to get into this right now, thank you.

Then he whistled. "Wow, you kind of look more like a dark angel now, Angel."

That nickname was never cute, nor accurate.

Leo said to Chance, "You know who she reminds me of? Angelina Jolie in that movie *Tomb Raider*."

Chance rubbed his chin. "Nah, it's more like Kate Beckinsale in *Underworld*. Except with strawberry-blonde hair."

Leo said, "I thought it was called *Van Helsing*?"

"That was another one. Same actress, though," Chance said.

"What ever happened to her?" asked Leo.

I sighed. "You forgot Xena."

"Xeeeeenaaaaaa," they both said slowly.

"If you two jacknuts are done..." I didn't wait for an answer but went straight toward the check-in area and grabbed the guest book and the day's receipts. The tigress image was still burned in my mind. Mother, hunter, protector. Was Maegan telling me that she would still protect her clan—her cubs—from beyond the grave? Or was she warning me that the Hunter was more dangerous than I could imagine and that I needed to prepare for a battle and—perhaps—a sneak attack?

If it meant saving Ivy, that was a no-brainer.

Bring. It. On.

I walked toward the door and called, "Thor! Road trip!"

The dog bounded down the stairs and started talking to me in that half-bark, half-growly sound that Great Danes make when they get excited.

"Where are you going?" Leo asked.

"Where's my truck?" Chance asked.

Cinnamon came downstairs then and said, "Cripes, you didn't tell him yet?"

So close. I slowly turned and Thor got jumpy, realizing we were going nowhere for the moment.

"It's on Crescent Drive, Chance. I had a little fender bender, but I swear I will pay for the damages."

Chance looked like I had just kneed him in the kumquats.

I walked over and said, "I'm sorry, I really am. And I want you to know I appreciate all you've done." I kissed him on the cheek and Leo shifted uncomfortably.

I walked over, kissed Leo on the cheek, and said, "And thank you for taking care of things here and for looking out for my family."

I left them standing there with their mouths open as Thor and I walked out the door. I hated to pull the flirtation card, but there was no way they were going to let me walk out of there without a million questions, looking as I did, and I just didn't have the time.

I was on a Mission from a Goddess.

Chapter 54

The shed was situated between the house and the cottage. Unfortunately, so was John. The man had impeccable timing. And by impeccable, I mean he was becoming a complete pain in my ass.

Thor trotted along behind me and the clang of the locket against the ring on his collar reminded me there were three pennies inside. One showed my birth year, one Ivy's, a third unknown.

Perhaps it was the birth year of the Guardian?

I ignored John, who was walking toward me, and opened the shed. Yep. All my furniture. Never should have said I was going out of town. Those vultures. Pimping out my house. To be fair, they did own it and the rent was dirt cheap, but still.

John came up behind me and said, "How's it going, Sweet Cheeks? Kill anyone today?"

"No." I bent down to shove some boxes aside. None were labeled *Blessed Book—Keep Away from Stacy*. "But it's still early." I stood up, looked around for my keys.

"Whoa, look at you. Let me guess, *The Housewives of Transylvania*." He laughed at his own joke and I chucked a pebble at him.

"That bar having a theme again tonight?"

"Sure," I said, because it very well could be.

"Leo at the house?" He thumbed toward the inn.

"I thought you were on your honeymoon. Isn't your bride a bit annoyed that you're spending all your time with your bromance?"

"Nah, she don't care." He pulled something from his pocket. "I just came by anyways cuz she found these in the kitchen drawer. They yours?"

I looked at the contents of his hand. "My keys! Thank you."

My keys. Deirdre had my keys? The keys to my office were on this key ring. And hadn't John said this morning that Deirdre had spilled a drink on Mr. Sayer while they were singing karaoke? That was why his shirt was wet.

Was she the Guardian? Had she discovered Sayer was a Hunter? If so, why hadn't she come forward?

Or was she a Hunter? She could have broken into my office if she had access to my keys.

John turned to go and I said, "Where is she? I'd like to thank her."

"She's out spending my money."

He turned again and I reached for his arm. "Wait a sec."

He faced me, one eyebrow arched.

I said, "You know, I just realized I never thanked you for everything you did. How about I buy you a cup of coffee?"

Maybe I could get some information from him. It wouldn't come easy. I couldn't just say, *So, John, is your wife a voodoo priestess or perhaps a Guardian of an ancient text?* But I could at least ask where they're from, maybe get her maiden name. Anything would be more information then I had now.

John smirked at me. "What, are we friends now?"

"It's just a gesture." I smiled. "I'll throw in a doughnut."

John said, "Thanks, but no thanks. I thought I'd grab a six-pack and catch a game." He headed for his car.

"I like football," I said. "I'll buy."

That was perhaps a bit too suspicious.

He stopped, tilted his head, and said, "What's with you?"

Gus pulled up then, looking like a pound puppy. Probably because his badge was missing. Leo was bound to come out of the house any second now.

"Forget it. Have a great day."

Thor and I hopped in the car and sped off.

We pulled up to Muddy Waters Coffee Shop a few minutes later for some octane. I reached back to check the pennies in the locket and jotted down the date of the one I had yet to identify. It was older than the other two.

Derek knocked on the window then. He made a drinking gesture and pointed to the coffee shop. I nodded and removed the door key from the ring so Thor could stay in the warm car. I climbed out and joined Derek in line.

Iris Merriweather greeted us. She was not only the local barista but the gossip columnist for the paper as well. She didn't get a lot of action because most people clammed up around her, but when she did sink her teeth into a story, you could bet it was the talk of the town for weeks. Mostly because that was all there was to talk about until the next juicy gem. She believed that people had every right to know if their neighbors were philanderers, cheats, ex-cons, or preferred paper over plastic.

I could only imagine the earful she was getting from the locals about the incident at the Geraghty Girls' Guesthouse this morning.

She placed our orders on the counter in front of us, her excitement literally spilling over onto my shiny black boots as the coffee sloshed. I grabbed a napkin and wiped up the spillage.

"Oh boy, I was hoping you two would come in. Wow, do we have a juicy one for the paper, huh?" She glanced from Derek to me, her glasses bobbing. "Love your outfit, Stacy."

Derek turned to me and said, "Yeah, who are you supposed to be, anyway? You look like my cousin Cindy when she got picked up at the Harley-Davidson store for selling crack."

"Remind me never to invite your family for Thanksgiving," I said.

"Oh, like you're one to talk." Derek paid for both our coffees and I thanked him.

Iris said, "So, I was thinking about some headlines." She babbled off three titles and I had to stop her at the last one. *Folks are dying for a night at the Geraghty Guesthouse.*

"Sounds great, Iris. You write them all down and send them to us, okay?"

She bobbed her head up and down, and went about filling the muffin tray. "All this and I get to cover the murder-mystery dinner. Should be a great weekend!"

Derek and I took a seat near the window so I could keep an eye on Thor.

"You going to that?" he asked, and sipped his coffee. A bit of whipped cream lingered on his lips and he wiped it off with a napkin.

I gave him my "are you kidding me" look.

"Right. Anyway, what have you got?" he asked.

Obviously, I couldn't tell him everything. But I didn't see the harm in mentioning the zombie powder, especially since his aunt had knowledge of voodoo. I wondered if he did too.

Then again, could I trust him? What if he somehow had something to do with this? Even though Derek seemed like a straight-up guy, naive even (he wasn't long out of college), I was wary of everyone then.

He said, "I take your silence for a complete strikeout, but that's okay." He pulled something from a satchel and laid a folder in front of me. "Because I got the nuts, baby."

I wrinkled my nose. "Have you been watching *The World Series of Poker* again?"

"You want to talk about that outfit?"

"Not especially." I really needed to at least wash my face. The jacket was covering most of the Xena belt, but there was just entirely too much leather involved to be taken seriously anymore.

Derek looked around, leaned in, and said, "Two words." He held up his first two fingers as if I needed a visual aid. "Zombie. Powder."

He slapped the table and leaned way back in his chair, tilting the front legs at an angle.

I sipped my coffee, not wanting to ruin his big reveal, but he caught on quick.

"Do not tell me you have heard of it, woman."

It used to annoy me when he addressed me like that, but Derek says it with an air of respect. Kind of like you might say "sir." Or "Mr. President."

"It's a powdered form of the toxin found in the puffer fish. Right?"

"Did you call the ME too?"

I nodded, and that seemed to make him feel better.

Derek launched into the phone call he had made first to the medical examiner, asking if there was a substance that could mimic death but allow the victim to survive. Then he called his aunt in New Orleans. "So she tells me how nasty this stuff is and that they use it in Haiti, where she's from." He gulped some coffee. "And she says, there is no way the doll and the zombie juice are a coincidence. She's pretty sure they are related. So what's our move?"

"What time does that dinner start, Derek?"

He asked Iris.

"Cocktails at seven, dinner at eight," she called.

It was nearly four now. The drive to and from the bank, barring little to no traffic, would take an hour and a half. That put the time at five thirty—if I left right now. Guests might still be in their rooms, readying for dinner, so I could chance that I could catch some of them for an interview when I returned. However, I still didn't know where the Honeycuts or the three girls had been rebooked. There were two hotels and seven B&Bs in town. Calling them all would take too much time.

For Derek, it was about a story. For me, it was so much more. But I couldn't tell him that, and I couldn't do it all myself. I thought of asking Cinnamon to help but quickly relinquished the thought. Subtlety was not my cousin's strong suit, and if anyone gave her an attitude she might ruin any chances of getting the information I needed to get Ivy back. And the clock was ticking. From my time spent in Chicago, I knew that the first twenty-four hours were crucial in any kidnapping, though I was certain she wouldn't be harmed. From what Birdie told me, whoever took her needed me too. And of course, the third in our little band of merry morons.

What worried me the most was I still hadn't received any contact from the kidnapper.

I sighed. I needed Derek's help. Trusting him was the only way.

"Come on," I said.

We said good-bye to Iris and she waved and said, "You kids should really think about coming to the dinner. The view of the river is so clear from the hotel."

I stopped, sucked in a deep breath, and grabbed Derek's hand. "It's tonight."

Chapter 55

"Yeah, it's tonight, we just covered that. You okay?" Derek asked.

I heard the words he was saying, but my mind was focused on another message. *The only clue I have uncovered as to where the attack will happen is this: The river is clear on this fateful night, though the Hunters are hidden well within sight.*

The murder-mystery dinner was to take place at the Riverview Hotel tonight, from which the Amethyst River could be seen. Every participant had a role to play. So of course, they would be hidden behind the identity of their characters.

Then a horrifying thought occurred to me. What if folks were parading around town via their character names, maybe even signed those names into the guest books? Hadn't Birdie said the instructions were sent via confirmation? What if the murder-mystery instructions said Mr. Sayer did it with a candlestick in the ballroom, but the man himself was named something else? Like Mahoney.

Maybe I should go to whoever was running the murder-mystery dinner to find out how it was organized, how it would be set up, and how it would play out.

"Get in the car," I told Derek.

He didn't question me, just did it. I drove to a quiet spot and pulled out the guest book.

No relocation information. "Dammit!" I did have receipts, though.

"You're holding out on me. I knew it!" Derek said, and Thor growled a low warning.

"It is not what you think. I promise. Look here." I handed him the guest book, searching for a way to explain my theories on Mr. Sayer's assault without mentioning the, ahem, family matters. "This is the list of guests who checked in along with Mr. Sayer last night. Maybe one of them slipped him the drug."

"My aunt says they put it in people's shoes. Or blow it in their face."

"Fine, maybe one of them blew it in his face. Also, he was out for a while at Down and Dirty. Talk to Monique and see who he was hanging out with, how long he stayed, et cetera. Call Gladys if you have to. She'll be glad to help with the data searches. Start her on the names from the credit-card receipts."

Gladys was the research assistant at the paper and a huge fan of Birdie and the aunts. Like little girls dream of being Taylor Swift, Gladys wanted to be a Geraghty Girl.

The Campbell party said just that in the guest book, and there was only one receipt, for Vivian Campbell, though I knew there were more women in their party. The Honeycut receipt indicated the first name to be Claudia. Right, a gift from their daughter. John and Deirdre paid in cash. So did Sayer. First name, Michael.

"What are you going to do?" Derek asked.

"I have to run an errand. Insurance companies." I rolled my eyes for effect. "You lose one guest and there's all kinds of red tape." I turned my head. Wow, that was almost believable.

"Okay, then. I'll keep you posted," Derek said and opened the car door.

"Wait a sec," I said. "Start with the Dinellis. John and Deirdre. He's an ex-cop from Chicago who investigates judges now. She's a court reporter. Leo and John go back a ways, so you can try to pump him for information if you have to."

"Anything else?"

I was about to say no when a thought occurred to me. "Actually, yes. Call your aunt. Ask her if there is anything that can combat zombie powder."

Derek gave me a funny look and then hopped out. A few seconds later, a text came from Cinnamon.

U ok?

I texted back. *Sure*

I don't believe u. Pick me up?

Oh no. I didn't want Cinnamon involved in this. Normally I was confident that my cousin could very much take care of herself, but this was something way beyond my comfort level. Even though I was better armed than a tank full of ninjas, I couldn't risk her getting hurt.

Can't. Outta town.

Liar.

??

Another text came in then. I pressed the ignore button and started the engine.

Cinnamon opened the passenger-side door of the car and said, "I'm in."

"I can see that. Now get out."

"No, I mean, I'm in. Whatever you're about to do, I want to help. Got a good nap, so I'm ready to go. And since I haven't slapped anyone yet today, I'm pretty wound up."

"That's what I'm afraid of. I don't want this to turn into a scene from *Rambo*."

"Is that a shot at my Italian heritage?"

"That's a shot at your anger-management problem."

She looked less offended. "I can accept that. Where we headed?"

"Cinnamon, I said no. Get out of the car."

"If you think I'm going to let you do"—she looked me up and down, her sunglasses perched on her nose, dark hair cascading down her shoulders—"whatever the hell it is you do when you're dressed like the Princess of Darkness, you're loonier than Lolly. And by the way, I'm driving." She scooted all the way over, forcing me to open the driver's door and tumble out of the car. I saw her twist her head to say something to Thor. His ears perked up and then he stretched out across the backseat.

I sighed and my phone chirped, reminding me I had a text as I walked around the car.

It was from Ivy.

Chapter 56

IVY GERAGHTY'S PERSONAL BOOK OF SHADOWS
by Ivy Geraghty

Entry #15

I am about to go all Krakatoa on someone's ass! That's right, bitches, you have messed with the wrong Warrior. Luckily, I managed to eat the Ogham note before they grabbed me (which was so not Snickers bar satisfying, let me tell you). My Geraghty instincts were on high alert. I sensed the Danger before I was taken. And as one of the chosen, I am sworn to protect The Secret, even with my notebook and backpack gone. Little do they know, I always carry pen and paper hidden on my person.

Hark! Do I hear? There is talk of moving me. Who is on the other end of the phone? I get to work calling on Petey and Moonlight.

—Ivy Geraghty, Prisoner of War

Chapter 57

The message read, *ten pm, river hotel.*

I had to try. Even though it was doubtful the text came from Ivy or even that an answer would come, still I had to try.

Who is this? I texted back.

Nothing.

It was close to four thirty then. I decided that Cinnamon driving might not be such a bad idea after all. I could remove the chaps and wipe the crap off my face, plus make a few phone calls.

I opened the door, leaned my head in, and said, "How soon can you get us to Havenswood?"

Cinnamon frowned at the dashboard. "In this pontoon boat that Gramps calls a Buick? Forty-five minutes, at least."

"Let's get your car."

Cin smiled wide at that and we made a quick stop at Panzano's Autobody to pick up the red Trans Am with the phoenix rising painted on the hood. I waited by the Buick with Thor as Tony scooted out from underneath a silver sedan. He smiled at the sight of his wife, his perpetually tanned skin marked with grease splotches. He stood up, wiped his hands on a red towel, and leaned in to kiss her.

I felt a pinch of jealousy at their solid relationship. They made it look so easy. I couldn't even hold on to a dry cleaner.

I plucked my phone from my pocket, called Iris, and asked who was in charge of the murder-mystery dinner this evening. She said it was headed up by Bea Plough, which was not good news. Bea Plough was on the board of the Convention and Visitor's Bureau for the town of Amethyst. Bea also taught Sunday school, which made my grandmother public enemy number one in her eyes. Despite the friendship between her husband, Stan, and my gramps, I was a bad seed.

Cinnamon grabbed a hoodie, zipped into it, then put her jean jacket over that. She trotted back and said, "Let's roll."

"I have to make a stop at the Ploughs' house first."

"What in God's name for?" Cin was not a willing participant in Bea's class. Her mother had insisted on her attendance until Bea tried to smack Cinnamon with a wooden paddle. Cinnamon had wrestled the paddle away from Bea, smashing a statue of a wise man in the process. She was not invited to return.

"I'll explain on the way."

The Ploughs' home was a two-story Federal brick set back from the road. I followed the cement walkway, stepped onto the porch, and cranked the old-fashioned doorbell.

Bea Plough answered. "Yes?" Her voice was firm, authoritative.

She didn't look happy to see me.

"Hello, Mrs. Plough. My name is Stacy Justice—"

"I know who you are, Stacy," Mrs. Plough said in her own special way.

"Of course. Excuse me. I was hoping I could ask you a few questions about the murder-mystery dinner event this evening?"

Bea pursed her lips and smoothed out her gray skirt. Her gray hair was knotted in a bun that rested on top of her pink scalp. "I'm very busy, Stacy. The dinner is in a few short hours and there is much to attend to. You can question me about it afterward for the newspaper. Good-bye." She shut the door in my face.

I cranked the bell again.

After a moment, the door creaked open.

"Yes?"

"Please, it isn't for an article, and it will only take a moment." I smiled—piously, I hoped.

"No." Slam.

Gave the bell another turn.

"What?" She was hostile now.

"May I at least see the instructions you gave to the participants?"

"No." Slam. Lock.

Oh, this bitch was asking for it.

Ring, knock, ring, knock. Ring! Knock!

The door opened again. "Stop that!"

"Look, lady, normally I would play this game all goddamn day just to watch you have a nervous breakdown, but I am in a bit of a time crunch. So knock off the bullshit and give me the fucking paperwork, or else I swear to Christ I'll draw a pentagram on your lawn so big it'll be visible from the Hubble Space Telescope. Then

I'll tell Iris that you've taken to dancing naked under the full moon."

Bea's face fell and I knew I had her. Those Sunday-school classes were her pride and joy, although I suspect more from the power the job granted her than the privilege to preach the message of her heavenly father. If word got out that she had switched teams, her post would surely be yanked out from under her.

"What's going on out here, Bea?" Stan said behind her.

"It's nothing," Mrs. Plough said over her shoulder.

"Mr. Plough!" I called.

"Who is that?" Mr. Plough came forward and his wife stepped aside. "Stacy?" He was a thin man with a thin mustache perched above thin lips. He reminded me a lot of Vincent Price. But maybe that's just because I always assumed living with Bea would be like living in a horror flick. "Hello, Mr. Plough. Your lovely wife was just offering me some information on the murder-mystery dinner."

"Well, certainly, come in. Bea, would you please get Stacy some tea?"

I held up my hand. "No, that's all right. I'm fine." She'd probably spit in it.

Bea said, "I'll just get that information for you, then." She disappeared for a moment and Stan commented on the weather, which he thought was clearing up. I thought a shit storm was coming, and I had no umbrella.

Bea returned, handed me an envelope, and said, "Here you go. Now, Stan, don't forget you need to drive me soon."

Stan said it was nice to see me and left. I didn't bother thanking Mrs. Plough as I turned to go.

I heard her say behind my back, "They should have locked you up along with your mother."

I stopped dead in my tracks. I must have looked strange because Cinnamon straightened up in her seat, staring at me.

I turned back. "Excuse me?"

Bea gave a sinister smile and creaked the door closed.

When I got back in the car, Cinnamon asked, "What's wrong? Did you get what you needed?"

I faced her. "She said something about being locked up with my mother. Do you know what she's talking about?"

Cinnamon faced the road and twisted the ignition key. "She's just a mean old bat, Stacy. Pay no attention to her."

I shook my head, clearing the negativity from my brain. "You're right. Let's go."

Cin pulled away from the curb just as I spotted the Jehovah's Witnesses a block up. I asked her to pull up next to them, and when she did, I leaned out the window and gave them the Ploughs' address.

Then we were on our way to the bank. On our way to discover what the key in Ivy's backpack would open.

Chapter 58

I have too much respect for the truth to drag it out on every trifling occasion.
—Mark Twain

Cinnamon's car smelled of lavender thanks to one of those tree-shaped car fresheners hanging from her rearview mirror. Lavender is supposed to have a calming effect, but when your cousin is flying down the highway at eighty-five miles per hour, even a morphine drip wouldn't settle the nerves.

The *Smokey and the Bandit* soundtrack was in the CD player, and I was white-knuckling the dashboard.

"'We got a long way to go and a short time to get there,'" Cin sang. "'Watch old Bandit ruuuuuun.'"

"Cinnamon, slow down! I don't want to die in this outfit!"

"Relax, I'll get us there."

I took a few deep breaths as Thor tried to stick his head out my window. I fumbled through the center console compartment and found a pack of tissues I used to wipe the gunk off my face. Then I took off the chaps and the nine-knives belt and tossed it in the backseat, saving one that I stuck in my boot.

The envelope Bea had handed me was on my lap so I opened that next. It contained the brochure for the dinner and a number to call for tickets. That was it. No instructions on how the game was played, nothing about character sheets or a list of attendees.

I decided not to draw the pentagram, but I would tell Iris that Bea Plough had once worked as a go-go dancer.

I recognized the number on the brochure as belonging to Gladys.

She answered on the first ring in that thick Polish accent of hers. "Ya?"

"Hi, Gladys, it's Stacy."

"Good to hear from you, Stacy. I get message from Derek. Am looking up information now."

"Perfect, Gladys. Listen, I hear you're in charge of the tickets for the mystery dinner tonight."

"Ya. I am Zelda woman. Reader of the balls."

"Excuse me?"

"You know, like fortune-teller. Is my character."

"Oh, you read crystal balls. Good for you." Because, really, who would want the alternative?

"You want ticket? Is half price."

"No, I don't want—"

"I make commission on tickets. Is good price."

"No, thanks, I—"

"Get cocktails, dinner, dessert, prizes."

"Fine, two tickets, Gladys." Anything to speed this along. I gave her my credit-card number as Cinnamon gave some guy the bird for honking his horn.

"So, Gladys, do you know anything about how the game is organized or who is in what role?"

"No. You come. Is surprise. You see."

Another call came through. Derek.

"Okay then, call me back when you finish the research."

"Ya. Bye-bye."

Derek didn't bother saying hello. "My aunt says the only counter effect to zombie powder is bat shit."

Of course. "Can you get some? I think they might have it at Glenda's Garden Shed. People use it to attract bats to their homes so they eat the mosquitoes."

"Hold up. First of all, I can't confirm her nutty theory with anyone. Not even on the net. Second, why the hell do you need it?"

"Just humor me. Bring it to the Riverview Hotel by six thirty."

Derek sighed. "I'll do my best. I found the other girls in the Campbell party. Anita Delaney and Kimberly Vaughn. They're staying at the Riverview now."

"Did you say 'Delaney'?" That was one of the clan names. Mahoney, Delaney, Geraghty.

"Yeah, but I checked them out. College girls. Lots of bikini and beer shots on Facebook. None of them work, none of them are Goth girls or even remotely threatening. Kimberly's favorite quote is, 'You can lead a horticulture, but you can't make her think.' Dorothy Parker."

"What about Anita?"

"She's pretty hot. She's got that Beyoncé thing going on. Her favorite quote is, 'Love is or it ain't. Thin love ain't love at all.' Toni Morrison. Sweet, huh?"

"Adorable. Find out all you can about her, okay? Then call me back." Delaney was a common name, but still, there was a good chance.

"Not a problem. I'm picking her up for a drink later."

"You sure that's a good idea?"

"Um, did you not hear me say she looks hot in a bikini?" Then he laughed. "Oh, you cannot think this little girl zombified a dude. Come on, Justice."

"Just be careful. Anything else? Anything on Sayer?"

"Nada. It's like the dude doesn't exist. The couple staying in the cottage are everything you said they were. He investigates judges and she's a court reporter. Although Deirdre spent a little time in a psych ward when she was a teenager."

That got my attention. "Do you know why?"

"No, the records are sealed on that, but a judge ordered her to undergo a mental-health evaluation after she beat the snot out of her boyfriend."

"Wow."

"Yeah, shattered the guy's jaw, which could have been a felony. She's a tae kwon do black belt. Anyway, I've got Gladys working on the other couple. I'll meet you at the hotel later. Peace out." He hung up.

Deirdre was a tae kwon do black belt?

Thor pierced through my thoughts with a long howl. His feeding call. And I had nothing to give him.

"Front-door service," Cinnamon said, and I looked up to see that we had made it to the bank fully intact.

I said, "Great. Thanks for driving. Listen, can you run and get Thor something to eat?"

Cinnamon loved Thor as much as I did, although she was far less patient with his antics. She gave him a rigid look and said, "If I do, will you stop bellowing?"

Thor licked her cheek.

"Fine. I'll pick something up and park in the back lot to feed him. Meet me back there."

I agreed and scooted out the door.

The bank was in a strip mall and it had that dull flat carpet that wears well but looks horrendous. The key was in my pocket as I approached a short teller with wide-set eyes and a ponytail. She could barely see above the counter.

"How may I help you?"

I smiled at her, not sure what to say. I've never had a safe-deposit box because I never had a need for one. Well, I never had a need for one before I learned that my family was the Secret Service for ancient texts of the Emerald Isle. Now I probably should invest in one.

"Yes, I need to access a safe-deposit box."

"Certainly. What's the number and I'll see if you're on the list."

Uh-oh. "List?"

Her name plate read "Tanya." "Yes. All the boxes have a list of names that are allowed access. So I'll need your identification and the number on the box."

"Oh, of course. Um…" I pulled the key out and she punched some buttons on her computer. "The number is 33299."

"And your name?"

"My name?"

What if I wasn't on there? Would they confiscate the key?

"I need your name, miss," she said calmly. "And ID."

A man walked over then and said, "Tanya, Mrs. Heff is in my line and she's insisting that you're the only one she'll give her account number to. Can you help her? I'll take this lady." He looked at me with warm brown eyes. "Why don't you step over here, miss?"

I followed his direction, trying to come up with a reason why I didn't know my name.

He held out his hand and winked.

That took me aback.

"Mrs. Smith, isn't it?" He raised both eyebrows and I nodded.

The key felt warm as I extracted it. I hesitated. Could I trust him?

Then he said, in the softest tone, "She said you'd come."

I handed him the key.

Brian was the name in front of his window. He grabbed a set of keys, escorted me to a door with a keypad entry, punched in some numbers, and the door slid into the wall. Then we walked through to an expansive room with little lockers lined up on top of and across from each other. There was a door inside that room too. Also with a keypad.

Brian walked over to the box number that matched the key, pulled out his set, and handed me mine.

"We both twist at the same time, so go ahead and insert the key."

I did and the door popped open. I pulled out a dull tin rectangular-shaped box.

Then Brian walked over and pressed some numbers on the keypad to the other door. He said, "You'll want privacy, I'm sure."

"Who said I would come? How do you know me?"

Brian shrugged. "I don't know you, but my manager, Mrs. Smith, showed me a picture of you and said you would come for her safe-deposit box. She said you were the only one authorized to open it. But she forgot to put your name on the list."

Or she left it off on purpose. Mrs. Smith. An alias? Or was Ivy's last name Smith? "Is she here? Mrs. Smith?"

Brian said, "No. Up and quit with hardly any notice a couple weeks ago. Right after that old guy came to visit her."

"What old guy?"

"I don't know who he was. Met with her in her office for a good hour. That day after closing, she told me about the box and how only you were to access it. Said if I did her this favor that she would make sure she left a glowing recommendation for me to replace her. And she did. She kept up her end of the deal, so I will too. You're lucky you got here when you did. We only stay open until five one Saturday a month."

"What does Mrs. Smith look like?"

Brian stepped back and I thought I had blown it. But he wasn't weighing his decision to grant me access to the box. He was checking me out.

He shrugged again. "A little like you, I guess."

I thanked Brian and stepped inside the privacy room with the box.

Chapter 59

IVY GERAGHTY'S PERSONAL BOOK OF SHADOWS
by Ivy Geraghty

Entry #16

My beloved Petey does not come. Perhaps it is that he only comes at night (or maybe my senses are dulled to whatever concoction they used to send me to la-la land). But Moonlight is close, I can feel it!

(Note to self, thank the big sis for giving up her cat.)

—Ivy Geraghty, Prisoner of War

Chapter 60

Inside the box was a map with a plastic cover encasing it. It looked incredibly old, yellowed, and fragile. There were mountains and roads with names I didn't recognize, and a long river cut through the center of the paper. At the foot of the river was a thick black X.

A treasure map? Was this what it was all about? A buried treasure? Birdie had said the first page of the Ballymote book had been destroyed, but maybe this was a copy.

In the Ogham code, our mother wrote that this was a token of insurance. I wasn't sure why, but I knew this might save Ivy's life. Or mine.

Now, who was the old guy? A member of the council, perhaps? Verifying Ivy as the Warrior? But then why would our mother flee?

Unless the man was a Hunter.

Brian knocked and said, "Closing time."

I slipped the map inside my jacket pocket. The left wristband was starting to itch, so I stuck my nail underneath and scratched. There was an odd tingling sensation as I did so, and both bands tightened, as did the bootstraps.

That was strange.

Brian led me out of the secured area and I thanked him for his help.

It was five o'clock when I stepped outside. Cinnamon's car wasn't in front, so I circled around to the back and scanned the parking lot.

It wasn't there either.

Where the hell was she?

I heard a crunching sound at my back and I whirled around to face Deirdre.

Startled, I jumped back and said, "What are you doing here?"

Deirdre said, "I was hoping you would come here."

There was only one car in the lot near the Dumpster and I recognized it as one that was at the inn. It must have been hers or John's. Deirdre was standing in front of it.

The area was eerily vacant. My senses were on high alert, and I could feel the cold steel of the blade tucked in my left boot.

I took another step back.

Deirdre took a step forward as two words ran through my head.

Black belt.

I was a fighter, but this woman could probably kill me with one kick. Ivy, on the other hand, would have a better chance. She knew martial arts. I knew how to run, but these freaking boots wouldn't help me there.

"Don't come any closer," I said.

Deirdre said, "I'm just here to make sure you followed instructions."

"What are you talking about?"

"You know exactly what I am talking about. Now, where is Ivy? I haven't seen her with you all afternoon."

That put me on edge. "Who are you?"

"You mean you don't know?"

I shook my head.

"I'm Ivy's—" She stopped instantly, gurgled, and her eyes rolled back in her head. She crumpled into the car door.

That's when I saw the blood on her chest. I dropped to the ground and scrambled toward her, swinging my head to see where the shot came from.

Deirdre opened her hand and dropped a piece of paper. I picked it up. She stirred then and said, "Go."

"Who are you?"

"Go...protect...her..."

"I can't leave you!"

Then another bullet whizzed past my head, making me reconsider that decision.

I opened the passenger door to her car, climbed in, and hauled Deirdre in after me. I reached across her bleeding body to shut the door just as the side mirror shattered into tiny pieces.

The keys were in her pocket and I didn't look back as I gunned it out of the parking lot, thinking that I had flunked the first rule of warfare.

Never bring a knife to a gunfight.

Deirdre opened her mouth, and I said, "Don't talk. I'll get you to a hospital."

I fumbled in my pocket for my cell phone. I didn't know the area that well. Had no idea where any hospital was, but we were right near the highway, so I hopped on and tried to put as much distance between me and the shooter as I could. My hands were shaking so bad, the steering wheel vibrated as I sped away.

I didn't drive fast enough.

The back window exploded and another bullet ripped into Deirdre.

She slumped forward. Motionless.

Then, another shot must have hit a tire, because I lost control of the vehicle and careened into a ditch. The sickening sound of metal crushing metal almost made me lose my lunch.

I didn't have time to think about where I was or how bad I was hurt. I had to escape.

Chapter 61

It was dark then, and the woods up ahead were thick as I ran, low to the ground. When I was sure no one was behind me, I placed the 911 call, telling the operator that there had been an accident on Highway 20. I said a silent prayer for Deirdre as I disconnected. I didn't want to think about how I would explain to John what had happened to his bride.

I didn't even know myself.

And where were Cinnamon and Thor?

I unfolded the paper Deirdre had slipped to me and used the light on my phone to read, hoping for another clue.

Dear Sister,

How the years fly by, but now the time has come for you and your young protégée to reunite. Watch over her when I cannot.

It wasn't signed, which irritated me to no end.

Sister? As in blood relative? Did that mean the woman who raised Ivy was not my mother? Or did she mean it figuratively?

Unless it was another family secret, which I was grow-ing ever so tired of.

Protégée. The word played in my mind. And then I saw the connection. Deirdre must have taught Ivy some of her skills. She was a black belt in tae kwon do, an art Ivy had mastered as well. But then wouldn't Ivy have recognized her at the cottage last night? Unless she was too young to remember her. It sounded from the letter that they had been estranged for years. On purpose? Perhaps a disagree-ment? Or had something happened that forced them to separate?

Was Deirdre the Guardian?

I charged through the woods as fast as my boots would carry me. They felt tighter, as if my feet and legs were swol-len beneath the leather. The wind had kicked up consid-erably, but I wasn't cold as I trudged through the gnarled branches and ice-coated rocks, snagging and tearing the sleeve of my jacket on a jagged limb. I had no idea if I was headed in the right direction, but I knew I wanted to get as far away from whoever had shot Deirdre as possible.

Finally, over an hour later, I pulled out my cell and tried to call for help, but there was no reception.

And then I saw her.

The white deer. Standing gracefully still as if she were waiting for me.

Her ears flickered and she blinked her almond-shaped eyes at me. Then she turned and bounded over a fallen log.

Instinct told me to follow.

She was only a few yards ahead of me, so I kept my sight on her as we made our way through the forest. In the distance, I heard the screech of an owl.

The deer's fluid movements reminded me of the watery haze of the moon. She was all beauty and grace as she led me through the thicket of hundred-year-old oaks. Her presence calmed me enough that I could clear my mind and just focus on getting to safety.

We moved along at a brisk pace, neither of us stopping. My feet were throbbing after two more hours had passed, but I forced myself to ignore the pain.

I tried to conjure a vision, tried to gain some clarity as to what to do now, but none came. The pentagram necklace was tucked in my jacket and I pressed it to my heart.

A message drifted through me then. Though I wasn't certain it was from Maegan, because the voice in my head was my own. It may have been a long-ago learned lesson.

Three things from which never to be moved: one's Oaths, one's Gods, and the Truth.

I wanted to shout out, but I didn't in case the killer was still hunting me.

The truth? That had been moved from me long ago. And this was not my oath, this was a family oath my ancestors had taken that I was now bound to.

And a woman was dead because of it.

And a young girl was missing.

I vowed then and there to end it. Breaking the cycle was the only way.

But first, Birdie had to know what I was about to do.

I stopped, patted the pocket where the map was, and checked my phone again. Still no signal.

The imposition of living in a rural area—less access to technology. And take-out food.

When I looked up, the white deer was gone.

Cold fear like I had never known gripped me. I was alone in a dark woods without any idea how far from home I was. It was eight o'clock, the dinner would be starting, and Derek was probably wondering where I was, bat guano in tow.

And as if I had conjured them up, three bats flapped above my head, fluttering through the tree branches, collecting their evening meal.

Which was promptly deposited on my head through the opposite orifice.

You would think that being shot at, watching a woman take not one, but two bullets, smashing the second car in the span of twelve hours, and losing my sister to a psychopath over something I had only discovered a short while ago would have broken me.

But alas, no.

What finally cracked my spirit was a bat crapping on my head.

Hot tears flowed down my cheeks suddenly, followed by seething anger. I screamed into the night air. "You can't leave me here, Maegan! No matter what you think of my decision. You can't leave your great-granddaughter stranded in the woods with a maniac on the loose!"

"Well, what in tarnation are you goin' on about, little lady?"

I spun around to see a man in a thick plaid jacket staring at me like I was an escaped mental patient.

He was holding a shotgun.

"Well, who you talkin' to?"

I stammered, "Um, no one. I'm…I'm…"

He cocked his head. "You lost or something?"

Or something. I nodded.

The man grunted. "Ain't no reason to go yellin' at the woods. You've already scared the goats half to death just traipsin' through the property. Thought it was them school kids come to mess with 'em again. So I grabbed Old Blue here for moral support." He shook the shotgun.

Realization dawned on me and I stepped forward to get a better look at him. "Mr. Shelby?"

He squinted at me. "Yeah, that's me. And you are?"

My gramps had sold Mr. Shelby the land for his farm forty years ago. "I'm Oscar Sheridan's granddaughter."

He chuckled. "You don't say. Look at you, all grown up. Well, come on, it's cold out here."

I followed Mr. Shelby out of the woods and into his home.

"Restroom's around the corner there. I'll put on more coffee."

I accepted the offer, did my business, and washed up.

When I got back to the kitchen Mr. Shelby said, "Never had three visitors in one day."

"Three?" I said just as Thor trotted in and pounced on me.

He covered me in doggy licks, his tail thumping so hard he knocked over a cat. The cat hissed and ran from the room.

"You two know each other?" Mr. Shelby asked.

Relief washed over me. Cin must be here too, although I couldn't imagine why. "Yes, um, I was looking for him, actually. That's why I was in the woods."

This lying thing was getting easier.

Mr. Shelby handed me a coffee cup. "Sugar is on the table there. Milk is in the fridge. I gotta tend to the herd, so you two just make yourselves comfortable. Feel free to call whoever you need."

He left. I prepped my cup, pulled out a chair, and waited for the coffee to brew. I was exhausted. I leaned my head back and closed my eyes for a moment.

When I opened them, Mr. Sayer was standing in the doorway.

Chapter 62

I screamed, leaped back against the counter. "Don't come near me." I bent my arm toward the boot and the knife practically jumped into my hand. The wristbands tingled.

Thor looked from me to Sayer, his face clouded with curiosity. He stood firm, his ears alert, waiting to see what would happen next.

"No, thanks, I already got one." Sayer pulled a knife from his own pocket. It was the same one that had been sticking out of his back this morning. "You look like hell." He crinkled his nose. "Is that bat shit on your head?"

What was happening?

"Sit down," he said.

"No."

"Those boots cannot be comfortable."

"They won't be when I implant one in your neck."

He threw his head back and laughed. He put the knife on the table, and under the glare of the kitchen light I could see that it was plastic.

"They told me you'd be tough. But you're also a pain in the ass." He pulled out a chair and sat, nodded to another chair.

I looked at Thor. He was studying my reactions.

"Who told you that I'd be tough?"

"The council."

"So then." Thoughts whizzed through my mind, "That means you are—" The pieces were locking into place.

"The Guardian. At your service."

I looked at Thor again. He still had the locket with the pennies dangling from his collar. I reached over to unclip it and checked the dates. My birth year, Ivy's, and another.

But his name was Michael Sayer.

"Toss me your driver's license."

The man at the table reached into his back pocket, and I tensed, grabbed the blade handle. He opened a billfold, extracted a card, and slid it toward me.

I quickly plucked it from the Formica.

Michael Mahoney. DOB 1958. The date of the third penny.

Son of a bitch. The Guardian.

I tossed his license back and said, "Well, you suck at it."

He ran a hand through his hair and said, "Tell me about it. It was supposed to be my younger brother, but he died."

"I'm sorry."

He shrugged, picked up his license. "It was a long time ago."

I poured coffee in my cup, offered some to Mahoney, and when he declined, I sank into a chair. Thor finally relaxed then. He curled up next to me on the floor.

"But there was blood on your shirt."

"Yeah, some idiot cut his finger on a shot glass at the bar when me and Deirdre were singing karaoke. Squirted blood all over my back."

His shirt was inside out now.

"What about the games? Playing dead—the murder mystery?"

He leaned back and said, "Figured I'd have some fun while I was waiting for instructions. Can't do anything without approval." He smiled impishly. "Like you said, I suck at it. But waking up in the morgue? That lit a fire under my ass."

It was all sinking in slowly.

"You know what they got me with?" he asked.

"Zombie powder."

"No shit? We talking a voodoo priest?"

"I was hoping you would know."

He shook his head. "All I knew was the city and a name. Geraghty."

"What happened to you? Where did you go?"

"I wandered around for a while, not knowing my own name. That's when Shelby picked me up. I just told him my car broke down. He gave me a meal, couple pots of coffee, and slowly the fog cleared. I offered to help wash off his goats as a thank-you, and it wasn't until I saw you sitting there that it all came back."

That's the plus side of rural life. People will always help a soul in need.

I asked him if he knew what "Mahoney money" meant. He didn't. Then I asked if he knew what we were protecting. He knew about the page but didn't know what was on it. I decided not to tell him about the insurance in my pocket.

Then a thought occurred to me. "You were singing with Deirdre. Do you know her?"

"Nah, just met her. Why?"

His eyes darkened as I revealed what had happened. "A nice lady like that. She didn't deserve that. Do you know who the Warrior is?"

I nodded. "I think Deirdre may have been her aunt. Or she may be my sister. I'm not exactly sure yet. Her name is Ivy. She's fourteen."

He tilted his head and said, "Are you shittin' me?"

"It gets worse. They have her." I told him about the threats.

Mahoney stood up, determined. He said, "Well, let's go get her."

Chapter 63

My phone finally caught a cell tower on the walk to the inn. I scrolled through my messages. There were quite a few from Cinnamon, wondering where I was. I texted her and told her I had Thor and that I was on my way to Birdie's. She messaged back that she got pulled over for speeding after picking up Thor's dinner, and thanks to the arsenal in the backseat (oops), it took far longer than it should have. She finally convinced the officer that the knives were for a stage play she was performing in. When she got home, after waiting for me for an hour and realizing I wasn't coming back, Thor took off, and she had been searching for him and me ever since.

Derek also texted, wondering why I wasn't answering his calls and to say that he couldn't find the bat guano and did I want him to scrape some off of random houses? I ignored that and dialed my voice mail. Leo called to say that he was heading to Chicago with John, that Deirdre had been in an accident and was being airlifted to a hospital in the city.

Oh, thank Goddess. She wasn't dead! I said a prayer, asking for her to pull through, and stuffed the phone in my pocket, shoving away a twinge of guilt for abandoning her on the highway.

It was nine p.m. when we got there. I had one hour until I was to collect Ivy at the Riverview Hotel, and I told this to Mahoney.

Fiona answered the door. "Mr. Sayer, how nice to see you."

No shocked expression, no hint of surprise, she just greeted him as if the dead rose every day in these parts. Geez.

To me she said, meaningfully, "Stacy, your grandmother is waiting for you upstairs." Then she frowned and said, "My stars, child, why do you always come here looking like something the cat wouldn't kill?"

There was simply no way to respond to that, so I didn't.

She asked Mahoney if he was hungry and he was. The two walked toward the dining room and I crawled up the stairs, preparing for the wrath of Birdie and more lectures on how the sky was falling. Thor followed me but then got distracted when he spotted an empty bed. He settled in for a nap as I repeated the whole picture frame–hidden doorway trick from earlier.

Birdie was pacing when I entered the room.

"Well?" she demanded.

My grandmother. Sharp and to the point. Like an ice pick.

"Really? No 'Hi, Granddaughter, glad to see you're still alive'? Just 'Well'?"

Birdie rolled her eyes dramatically.

I said, "You want the good news or the bad news?" I hopped on top of the round table. The look on her face said she didn't appreciate me disrespecting her furniture. I hoped the look on mine said I didn't give a flying monkey's ass.

"Okay, let's start with the good." I clapped my hands. "I found the Guardian. Interesting turn of events, I must say. You would think that the almighty council in their infinite wisdom would appoint some hot guy built like a barbarian with dreamy eyes and defiant hair, but no. They chose a beer-guzzling middle-aged moron who managed to take a hit off a puffer fish."

Birdie looked surprised. "Mr. Sayer?"

"Mr. Mahoney," I corrected.

She nodded. "I see."

"Oh, but wait! It gets better. Because it's not really a party until someone gets shot."

I let that sink in for a few seconds.

She didn't blink. Just said, "Leo called. I am aware of the situation."

"The situation? Is that what we're calling it? I was shot at, Birdie, and Deirdre is fighting for her life because of it. That bullet was surely intended for me. And let's not forget that a fourteen-year-old girl is being held hostage by heaven knows who and I still don't know what it's all about!" I was talking so fast, spit flew from my mouth. The more I talked, the more livid I became.

"Do you know who Deirdre is?" she asked.

The question came as a surprise. "No. Why? Do you?"

"I spoke with the council. She was the original Warrior, but then she did something stupid that brought much attention to herself. Got herself arrested and seriously injured a boy. So she was stripped of the position. Ivy is her replacement."

Right, Derek's story about Deirdre shattering her boyfriend's jaw. "Are they related?"

"I can't say."

"Can't or won't?"

She sighed. "What I mean is, I do not know the answer to that."

I wasn't sure if I believed her, but enough was enough. I slid off the table and stood, not caring about what she wanted, what the council wanted, or what was expected of me any longer.

She asked, "What was in the safe-deposit box?"

"A lottery ticket." If she could play games, then so could I.

Fiona stepped through the opening then.

"I will ask you one more time," Birdie said in an unwavering tone. "What. Was. In. The. Box?"

"And I will ask you one more time. What is the secret, Obi-Wan?"

Fiona said, "She has earned it, Birdie."

Birdie whirled around to her sister and shouted, "She lost the Warrior."

"Two, in fact." I don't know why I said it. It just slipped out, but it certainly didn't help my case.

"But she found the Guardian, Birdie. He's in the dining room right now eating a baloney sandwich."

Seriously, who chose him?

I walked around both of them and said, "It doesn't matter anymore. This ends tonight. I'm going to make the exchange."

"You will do no such thing, Anastasia!" Birdie said.

The hell I won't. "I'm going to get my sister, Birdie, and that is that. Game over."

I was about to storm out, but the exit was gone. "Dammit, Birdie, put the door back."

She didn't speak for a while as I glared at her.

Finally she whispered, "She isn't your sister."

I said, "Excuse me?"

She repeated herself.

"And how do you know that?"

Fiona looked away as Birdie said, "Because I know where your mother is."

Chapter 64

I waited fourteen years for my mother to return. Fourteen years of graduations, boyfriends, jobs, birthdays.

Fourteen years wondering if I was an orphan—or just abandoned.

I steadied myself, trying to gain composure so that I wouldn't slap my grandmother. "Birdie, you had better not be serious. Because if you have known where she was all these years and you didn't tell me, I don't think I could ever forgive you." My voice didn't crack, even though there was a lump in my throat.

"Sit down, Stacy," she said softly.

Birdie never called me that, despite the fact that it was indeed my given name. Anastasia is something she made up to annoy my mother because Birdie felt it was bad luck to name a female child after her father.

Given the current predicament, maybe she was right about that.

I filled my lungs with all the air in the room and blew it out slowly. "I'll stand, thank you. Get to the point. I only have forty-five minutes."

She bowed her head for a brief moment, then spoke. "As you know, all Geraghty women are born with a gift. From the moment you came into this world, I knew you were powerful. It radiated all over your tiny pink body. I was delighted for you, for the opportunities you would have to make a difference in the world. So few people get that in life. Fewer still take the risks required to inspire change, but you were a fighter from the get-go. You learned everything early, and your gift was there right from the start. Even in your crib, you would babble away at the walls and I knew you were talking to the ancestors. Sometimes, I think they may have taught you even more than your mother and I did. You took to magic as if it were as natural as the air you breathed."

Watching her wax nostalgic was both unsettling and heartwarming. My grandmother was simply not the bread-baking, knee-bouncing, drawing-hung-on-the-fridge type.

"At first, your mother was as excited about your talent as I was, but then *her* gift grew stronger and, somehow, it transformed to focus only on you."

"What was her gift?" I couldn't believe I didn't remember, but I had buried all of that so deep down that not everything had resurfaced.

"She could see events before they unfolded." She paused and took a sip of water. "You cannot imagine how awful it was to watch her suffer through every scraped knee she couldn't prevent. Every tear she knew would fall but couldn't be there to dry. It was a nightmare with no escape, and it nearly drove her insane. There were times when I insisted she go away for a bit. The distance seemed to ease the visions, but then they would come back stronger. Of course, those trips sparked rumors of mental hospital stays, but she was at a spiritual retreat."

Locked up with your mother. That's what Bea meant.

She leaned in, took my hand, and said, "And then your father died, and more than ever she was desperate to keep you safe."

Tears welled up in my eyes then, but I fought them back.

"And then the worst vision of all came. You were fourteen and the council had verified you as the Seeker. Your mother didn't tell me until it was over, but she saw a vision of a man taking you. Then she saw your lifeless body."

I leaned in closer.

"She did not hesitate, did not discuss it with me even, she just acted."

"What did she do?" I asked.

"She took his life, before he could take yours."

I sat back, stunned. "My mother murdered someone?" My brain was fogging over, trying to wrap itself around what I just heard. But I didn't recall a trial, or even any rumors of a crime. Surely people would have known in this tiny hamlet. I said this to Birdie.

"The matter was not taken care of via the court system. You see, the man she killed was a member of the council. Her sentence was passed down via Celtic law."

"Where is she, then?"

Birdie paused, glanced at Fiona. "She is serving her punishment on the old soil. You cannot contact her just yet. But I am hoping when this—your first quest—is over, I can prove to the council that the measures your mother took to ensure your safety were in the best interest of all. With that, her release is imminent and your path will continue."

I shot her a confused look.

Birdie smiled. "Your gifts are great, and with great gifts come great challenges. In time, you will hone your skills to be prepared for any task that comes." She squeezed my shoulders, looked deep into my eyes. "You have to understand that she begged me not to tell you what she had done for fear that it would ruin you."

Her absence nearly did ruin me. All those nights I cried myself to sleep, thinking my mother didn't love me. The memory made me shudder.

"Why are you telling me now, then?"

"Because I wanted you to understand the importance of this. It isn't just about the book. It's about my daughter and my granddaughter. You must trust me."

I stood up, weighing everything she had said. Fiona was wearing a poker face, but I saw love in her eyes. And truth. Birdie was telling me the truth, and how could I blame her for hiding it from me? The gravity of it all came crashing down, and I felt the fight rise within me again.

With my mother's freedom at stake, there was only one thing to do.

Bluff.

"I will trust you, Birdie, on two conditions. First, you tell me what was on the first page of the Ballymote book. As Fiona said"—I flicked my eyes to my great-aunt—"I have earned it. And two…" I pulled the map from my pocket, set it on the table. "You tell me what this is."

Fiona and Birdie both read over the map, their eyes wide as saucers.

Fiona gasped, "It isn't—"

Birdie said, "No, but it's a good replica and altered well enough to work."

"Hello?" I tapped the table. "Seeker of Justice here, impending doom and all that, so can you please let me in on what we're staring at?"

"Insurance," Birdie said, and smacked her hands together, a mischievous look on her face. "Think about it, Anastasia. What does the Book of Ballymote open with? What is the first thing the reader sees?"

"A drawing of Noah's ark."

Fiona nodded, excited as a schoolboy who just discovered boobies.

Chapter 65

IVY GERAGHTY'S PERSONAL BOOK OF SHADOWS
by Ivy Geraghty

Entry #17

So they moved me to the crapper and I managed to take off the blindfold. I hear whispers behind the door, but it is barricaded. As my senses return, muffled sounds of shuffling this and that filter through the door. The voices are low and I cannot determine the nature of the conversation, but I hear the word *professor.* There is more than one voice, a man and a woman. The window is old and I manage to pry it open an inch, then two, but cannot fit through. I search and call for Moonlight, for my sister.

No one comes.

—Ivy Geraghty, Prisoner of War

Chapter 66

"Birdie, are you telling me that the secret we are supposed to be protecting is a map that leads to the location of the ark that Noah built?"

She grinned.

"You're serious? Noah's actual ark. It's not like a replica built by some Irishman who hit the absinthe a little too hard or anything, is it?"

She smirked at me, crossed her arms, and said, "Don't be ridiculous."

"Well, give me a minute here, Birdie. I am trying to wrap my brain around the fact that you—that anyone—would want to keep hidden one of the most significant artifacts of the ancient world." I started pacing, trying to catch up with the laps my mind was running. "I mean, think of the importance of this. Of the value it would bring to people. Especially the country where it's located." I stopped, looked at her. "Do you know where it is?"

She ignored the question.

"Birdie, it belongs to history, to scholars, to archaeologists. To the people who will preserve and truly protect it."

Birdie crossed over to the fireplace and it erupted in flames. I didn't see her strike a match.

I said, "It's the right thing to do."

"Ah," she said, her back to me. "And I suppose you know what is right for the entire globe? For generations to come and generations past?" She turned to face me, draped her arms out wide. Her cloak caught a spark, but with a snap of her fingers it was extinguished.

Okay, now she was freaking me out.

"Would you just tell me already? Why isn't it a good idea to present it to the world?"

She paused for a time, lifting her head skyward as if I asked these silly questions just to torture her.

Then she spoke. "Fifty years before Christ, the people and the government of Rome worshipped an ancient pantheon of deities. The empire was growing, spreading across Europe and other continents as the Romans conquered more and more land and people. Societies were expected to fall in sync with the laws of their new rulers. They were expected to forgo their own belief systems and instead blend into the Roman way of life."

"When faiths collide, blood is shed," said Fiona.

"Which is what happened when sects of Jewish people practicing what they called Christianity were discovered under the new empire."

Fiona said, "Power may strengthen armies, but it weakens minds."

Birdie nodded in agreement. "As the empire stretched further and further, infrastructures were built, connecting people who would not encounter each other otherwise. People who had heard Christ preach relayed his message to their new neighbors. When Constantine conquered both the east and west banks of Greece, he discovered that many social powerhouses were Christians. He needed their support, so he decided it would be in the best interest of the empire to claim one religion and declare it the law of the land."

"I recall studying that. It was 313 AD. Right?" I asked.

Birdie smiled. "Yes. It was also the beginning of a new way to govern—the integration of church and state. The first order of business was to persecute those identified as dualistic Christians—Gnostic Christians, Mithraic Christians, and so on."

"Then the pagans became the persecuted," said Fiona.

"So what does this all have to do with the ark?" I asked.

Birdie sat down on the settee. "The ark is a legend known across many faiths. Judaism, Islam, Christianity, each claiming the story, each still fighting wars in the name of their god." Birdie looked at me steadily. "It was agreed long ago that until the bloodshed ends—until people and governments cease to fight in the name of any deity—the ark is to remain lost to the ages."

I sunk into a chair. It was hard for me to recall a time when the words *holy war* weren't mentioned daily in the news. What she was saying made sense. Still, I wasn't sure it was the answer. People have been slaughtering each other in the name of faith for thousands of years. What would change by keeping this secret?

Then again, what would happen if it were discovered?

Suddenly a sharp pain pierced my forehead and images slammed through my mind, one after the other. Billowing clouds of black smoke choking the sky, exploding glass, people screaming, running, firefighters caked with debris and dust, babies crying, women leaping off high-rise buildings.

"Maegan, stop," I whispered.

I knew what she was showing me—knew the date, the day, the time.

When I looked up, my grandmother and my aunt were carefully reading my face. They were right. The world wasn't ready.

"I just have one question," I said. "Is this King Arthur's round table?"

Fiona said, "We bought that when the Renaissance restaurant closed, dear."

Fair enough.

Chapter 67

I left Thor sleeping on the bed on my way back to the dining room. Lolly was wearing a long orange-sequined ball gown that looked like it was designed by Elton John. A fuchsia shrug covered her shoulders, and she was wiping down the table.

"Lolly, where is Mr. Sayer? I mean, Mr. Mahoney."

She smiled at me with all her teeth and said, "He stepped outside for a cigarette." Then she held up a bottle and said, "Champagne?"

"No thanks."

I went to the front door and swung it open. Didn't see him, but Moonlight was there on the porch. I walked all around the property, but still there was no sign of Mahoney. Moonlight was close on my heels. Finally, he jumped on my shoulder and screeched loudly in my ear.

"Okay. Guess we'll need to do this without him."

The white cat followed me all the way to the hotel. I was banking on the fact that the knife in my boot and the map in my pocket would be enough to end this. After all, that's what they were after, not me, not Ivy. They wanted the book to decode the page, but I had something even better. I had what appeared to be the actual map.

My phone buzzed just as I got to the entrance. It was Gladys. "I try and try, but you don't answer phone."

"Sorry, Gladys. What have you got for me?"

"Claudia Honeycut is army soldier."

"Is she deployed?"

"What is this?"

"I mean is she fighting now? Is she overseas?"

"Oh. No."

I thanked her, disconnected the call, and stepped into the lobby. It was an old building, one of the oldest hotels in the state. The lobby was wallpapered in a floral Victorian-era print, the carpet a rich burgundy pattern. Past the tea cart loaded down with coffee and cookies was a wide, winding walnut staircase that led to the rooms upstairs. To the right of the lobby was a lounge, Ye Old Time Saloon. I poked my head in and saw Derek sitting at the bar next to a gorgeous woman who actually did have a Beyoncé thing going on. I debated whether or not to interrupt his date. Chose not to.

To the left was the grand ballroom. The lights were dimmed in there, and it looked as if the dinner was winding down. A DJ announced that the staff was about to spread the tables apart for dancing and that guests were invited to enjoy cocktails and live music. I could hear the clang of drum cymbals as band members set up on the backstage.

I walked up to the young desk clerk, who was reading a magazine, and asked if there was a message for me. Gave him my name and said I was meeting a friend who was a guest. There wasn't. He asked me the name of the party, and I hesitated.

Which name should I give?

Then, out of the corner of my eye, I saw Moonlight flick his tail. I turned to catch him running up the stairs.

I told the clerk that I'd just remembered the room number, and he shrugged and went back to reading. Then I followed the cat. My wristbands started itching again and I shook my hands for relief. They vibrated, then tingled, as did the boots.

I bumped into Mahoney drinking a beer at the top of the staircase.

"Hey, where you been?" he asked.

"What are you doing?" I hissed, pointing to the bottle in his hand.

He looked at the beer. "It calms my nerves."

"Where the hell did you go?"

He shrugged. "I had to take a leak."

I didn't even bother explaining that there was indoor plumbing at the house. I just called him an idiot.

"So this is where we're supposed to get the Warrior? Which room is it?"

I frowned. "I don't know." It was a quarter to ten. Time to make an executive decision, since clearly I was now the captain of this ship of fools.

"Go downstairs and ask which room the Honeycuts are staying in."

Brian from the bank had said an old guy had visited his former manager. It didn't make a lot of sense, and certainly a man in his eighties (or so he had appeared) couldn't have been chasing me down on the highway while shooting at us, but it was worth a look. He was the last of the guests that could have slipped Mahoney the zombie powder.

Unless his wife did.

Mahoney turned and trekked down the stairs, and I searched for Moonlight. I spotted him at the end of the long corridor, just turning a corner.

I chased him down, and up ahead there was Mr. Honeycut ambling along, a bucket of ice in his hands.

Then the vision flashed again. A woman tied to a bed.

That clinched it. If I was wrong, I would most likely be headed for prison, but when you're the Seeker of Justice and your mother is being held captive Goddess knows where; your sister is no longer your sister, but she's still in danger; and the only backup is in the form of a sweaty, potbellied bozo with all the intelligence of your average houseplant, you have to make swift choices.

It took two strides to reach him. I grabbed the dagger with my left hand, stuck it to his back, and horseshoed my right arm around his throat.

He squeaked and dropped the ice bucket, and I said, "Where is she?"

"The Seeker, I presume?"

"Listen to me, you son of a bitch. I have not had a good day. I wrecked two cars, ran in three-inch heels through a damp forest, got shot at, and I'm pretty sure I'm in the throes of PMS. Just take me to Ivy or I swear to God I'll stab you in both kidneys."

He tensed. "You got shot at?"

"Don't make me repeat myself. Take me to the girl or lose a lung. Your choice."

Honeycut slipped a key card into the door we were standing in front of, and it popped open.

I told him to turn the lights on, and he did.

Mrs. Honeycut was sitting on the sofa knitting. She looked up and greeted her husband. Then she turned to me, scowled, and said, "I don't see a book."

I said, "Do you see the six-inch blade in my hand? Kind of changes the dynamic of the situation. Put the knitting needles on the table, Mrs. Honeycut."

She did.

"Now," I said as I patted Mr. Honeycut down and found no weapons. "Where is the gun?"

I wouldn't call for Ivy until I knew she was out of danger. If she was even here, although I suspect the chair propped under the door across the room was a good indication she was.

Mrs. Honeycut furrowed her brow together. "What gun?"

Mr. Honeycut said, "She said someone shot at her, Cece."

"Who would do such a thing?" she asked, incredulous.

I said, "I'm going out on a wild limb here, but I'd say people who kidnap a defenseless child might not be gun-shy."

"Nonsense," Mrs. Honeycut said and stood up. "We don't believe in guns. And the child is fine."

Mr. Honeycut spoke then. "She's telling the truth. We may dabble in poisons but never firearms."

"We're scientists," Mrs. Honeycut explained, as if that made everything okay.

Someone knocked then and I heard Mahoney's voice just as the band started to play. The music was so loud, the floor shook. I ordered Mrs. Honeycut to open the door, still holding the knife to her husband's back. She did and Mahoney entered, eating a Snickers bar.

I directed Mrs. Honeycut to lie on the bed.

Mahoney said, "These are the Hunters? Ma and Pa Kettle?"

Mr. Honeycut extended his hand and Mahoney was just about to shake it when I said, "Don't do that."

He gave me a curious look, then said, "Oh yeah. Which one of you slipped me the goofy juice?"

Mr. Honeycut said, "Your ID fell out when you opened your wallet to pay at check-in. Remember, Mr. Mahoney?"

"Okay, I need some answers," I said. "First, who are you and how do you know about us?" I told him to sit next to his wife.

When he had settled onto the bed, he said, "Fifty years of research, my dear. I am the professor of ancient religions at the University of Chicago. The Ballymote book has been a fascinating mystery to me for decades. All the times it was lost and found, then lost again. I knew something in it had to be incredibly valuable. And just when I discovered what must have been on the missing page, a true Delaney walked into my classroom." He paused, as if picturing the scene in his mind.

"She was entranced by the story, devoured everything she could about it—more than any other student I ever had. It was obvious that it was personal to her. Once I had her school records, it was easy to trace her lineage." He looked at me, wildly. "Then it was a matter of keeping track of her, following her, watching her. And when her daughter came along, I studied her too. Her training was so intense she could only be the Warrior. The legend was true! I knew if I was patient, they would lead me to it and not only would that discovery change the world, but my name would go down in history as the man who located Noah's ark." He was breathing heavily now and I thought he might have a stroke.

"But then I made a mistake. I went to talk to her, to simply convince her that the ark belonged to the world." He looked at his wife. "You were right, Cece, I spooked her." Then he looked at me. "She fled after that, but I tracked her down, then followed her daughter here. And lo and behold, there was a Geraghty Guesthouse. I thought if we could get inside, we could search for the family book, which I suspect may hide the page, but we didn't find it."

"And so you broke into my office and searched there," I said.

He nodded, trained his gaze at Mahoney. "When we found you in our room, I was certain you knew what we were there for. I didn't want anyone to get hurt, you see, so I slipped you the toxin to keep you out of the way. I felt you were the biggest threat. A man, further along in life, wiser."

I rolled my eyes. "You have got to be kidding me. This guy?" I thumbed toward Mahoney.

Then I had one more question. Where was Ivy's mother?

Before I could ask it, Mahoney smiled and said, "Well, pops, you were right about that."

He took out a gun and shot them both in the head.

Chapter 68

Although prepared for martyrdom, I prefer that it be postponed.
—Sir Winston Churchill

Holy. Mother. Freaking. Shit.

"Why did you do that?" I rushed to the bed, but they were both dead.

I whirled back to Mahoney and said, "Answer me!"

He was on the phone. "It's done." Then he hung up. I grabbed the phone on the desk and Mahoney reached over and yanked the connection from the wall. Then I reached into my pocket and pulled my phone out.

"Drop it," he said. "The knife too."

"I'll never find her now. Ivy's mother is tied up somewhere, Mahoney!"

He smirked. "You think I give a rat's ass?" He ripped the line from the phone, strung it through his hands.

Ivy. Was she in the bathroom?

Then the door opened, and if I didn't believe in the Amazon tribe before, I did then.

The woman standing before me was well over six feet tall and looked like she could give a plow horse a run for its money.

This was so not good.

She smiled at Mahoney, kissed him, then looked at the bed and said, "Well, Daddy, you always said it was a quest worth dying for. I guess you got your wish." She laughed.

I looked at the man standing next to her. "I take it you are not the Guardian."

How could I have been so wrong?

They both laughed at that.

"You know, I didn't even believe that old coot until he asked me to book him a room as an anniversary gift." She walked around the bed and shook her head at her father. "All he cared about was that stupid book. Never made it to a birthday party, never came to a wrestling match. Just that stupid book!" She kicked him and I blanched. "And now that I know what's in it, can't say I blame him." Her eyes filled with fire. "Must be worth a fortune!"

"Well, you almost blew that now, didn't you, Claudia?" what's-his-name said.

"I'm sorry, Michael. When I didn't know what had happened to you, I panicked."

"You're also a terrible shot," he said, and kissed her. Then he looked at me. "She was aiming for you."

"Yeah, I got that."

"Sure, with that dinky gun. Now, give me an M16 and I'll hit my mark every time." She looked at me and said, "I figured whatever was in that bank you went to was the key."

Suddenly, the map in my pocket felt like an anchor.

"The bank was closed," I said.

Mahoney pointed the gun to my head and I really wished I had one of my own. I put my hands up.

"You sure about that?" he asked.

Adrenaline pumped through me as I thought about what to do. They would kill me either way, I was sure. The boots tingled around my ankles as I said, "I do have something for you. But you'll need me to interpret it."

Michael said, "Let's see it."

"It's in my jacket pocket. Left side."

When he reached in, he lowered the gun enough for me to act.

I launched into a full tackle, put all my weight behind it, and took him to the floor. His entire body twitched and lurched and the gun slid away. I felt a jolt as I leaped off of him and saw my wristbands flash like lightning.

Like Tasers.

The asshole was still flopping like a fish when I twisted around to find Claudia reaching under the bed. I jumped on top of her too, but I didn't have enough juice left to zap her, so basically, I gave her a bear hug. Her left fist connected with my nose and I flew back into a lamp, blood gushing all over me. Then Claudia screamed, did some sort of eggbeater move with her legs, and popped up with Moonlight glued to her face, scratching, clawing, ripping her flesh apart.

I forced myself up, heading toward the bathroom door to retrieve Ivy and get the hell out of there, when the door pulsated from the inside like someone had taken an ax to it. The chair propped beneath the knob splintered, and with another crack the door went down. Then Ivy came into the room, blazing.

Michael was back on his feet, ready to lunge, but Ivy put a stop to it with a leaping twist and a roundhouse kick to the chest, delivering an uppercut for good measure. He flew back across a table and slid to the ground. She took a stance against Claudia and they looked like David and Goliath for a moment. Then Ivy charged at her with a battle cry and a succession of front and side kicks, all of which Claudia managed to block.

My hand was on the dagger before I felt a stinging pain in my back. I fell to my knees and the dagger slid under the door and into the hallway. I screamed and reached behind me, pulled the knitting needles from my back. Michael jumped on top of me, slammed my head into the floor, and I planted a needle in his hand. He cried out and let go, and I flopped over.

I could see Ivy was holding her own against Claudia, but the woman was so much bigger. I worried one punch could knock her clean out.

Then she jumped on the bed, did a backflip, and caught the ceiling fixture. She curled her knees to her chin and like a jack-in-the-box sprang both feet out, planting them directly in Claudia's face. Three teeth flew from Claudia's mouth, and I was in such awe I forgot about my own attacker.

He came at me again while I was on my back, so I took a page from Ivy's book, curled my knees to my chin, and fired my legs at him.

As I did, I heard a sound like a firecracker.

Michael stumbled, grabbed his stomach, blood spreading across his shirt.

My boots were smoking.

Did I just shoot someone?

He fell back and Claudia screamed, lunged at me.

Ivy jumped on top of her and got a helicopter ride as Claudia tried to spin her off, but she was like a Velcro monkey and the woman couldn't shake her.

I scrambled under the bed for the gun but came up empty. Then I grabbed the phone cord, thinking I could tie her up, until I saw Claudia stand erect and slam Ivy into a wall. She whirled to face her opponent and the two commenced fighting.

I was desperate, running out of options. I took a long shot and pulled the nightstand drawer open.

Talcum powder.

But could it be? "Ivy, catch!"

She ducked a right cross, caught the powder, and I said, "Sprinkle it on her!"

She did not question, just did it. A brief look of terror crossed Claudia's face before she went down like a redwood.

Ivy dropped the powder and ran to me, gave me a giant hug. She high-fived me and danced a little jig.

"Whoo-hoo, we kicked ass! Did you see that uppercut I gave the dude?"

"Yes, Ivy." I opened the door, edged her out, me close behind.

"And you were awesome, sis! Are those magic boots?" She turned back and suddenly her eyes grew big and she said, "Look out!"

I turned just as Michael blew the powder in my face.

I slapped at it immediately with both hands, but nothing was happening. Then I recalled the bats in the woods.

Michael was stunned when nothing happened.

Which gave me enough time to plant my boot in his neck.

It didn't go off that time, but it did the trick. His eyes rolled back in his head and he fell on top of Claudia.

We slammed the door and ran down to the lobby. I had to thank Derek about the guano tip and invite his aunt to Thanksgiving.

Chapter 69

Four months later...

They found Ivy's mother, Anna (Delaney), in another room of the hotel, tied and gagged as in my vision. She had hair just like her daughter. Apparently they used the same brand of dye—Hot Tamale something or other.

She explained to me later that when Honeycut came to visit her, it was clear the hunting season had arrived. And so she did what any mother would. She used herself as a decoy to draw them away from Ivy. It worked for a time, until Honeycut realized that she would never give up her daughter. So he kept her in the room of the hotel and trained his sights on Ivy.

The map, she thought, would buy us some time if it was needed. If it reached a point of desperation. However, she knew that had she given it to him the day he came to visit, he would have realized, after studying it closely, that it was a forgery of the real map—the destroyed page of the

Ballymote book. There is strength in numbers, she told me, so she sent Ivy to the Geraghty clan. In her overactive fourteen-year-old mind, Ivy assumed she was a Geraghty.

"Because no one is really named Smith," she had said.

When she left Amethyst, Ivy took Moonlight with her. Cats choose their people, and Moonlight knew he was Ivy's familiar. Fiona had a little talk with him before they loaded him up. He'll keep her safe.

There have been a few phone calls, texts, and postcards exchanged. With each one, a nagging feeling tugged at my heartstrings, telling me that she would soon be leaving my life. Anna's caution had kept them moving around Chicagoland long before I met Ivy. Now it carried them farther and farther away to different cities, different states. Her greatest fear was that her daughter would always be in danger. Every second of every day.

And she would be.

The last time we spoke, Ivy promised me that the minute she turned twenty-one, she would come for a visit just to sit front and center at Monique's bar so we could take turns razzing her.

I pointed out that her age had never stopped her before, but it sounded like a fantastic idea.

The hearing to determine the fate of my mother was scheduled for Samhain. Birdie was working on pushing the date up, but since that's the beginning of the New Year according to the pagan calendar, apparently that was when the council decided the fate of the damned.

I thought it was bullshit and planned to tell them the first chance I got.

Michael didn't make it. Apparently, the boots were packing and the wristbands were indeed Tasers. Fiona explained that Lolly went hog wild in the spy store and maxed out her credit card to suit me up for whenever I would need it. I told her that information may have come in handy before the very bad man tried to snuff me. She was afraid I wouldn't wear them if I knew, and I must say, she was probably right. Mostly because I wouldn't trust a weapon Lolly had picked out.

Claudia went insane. Due to the zombie powder or just the fact that she was already a few gallons short of a full tank, no one could say. I was told her straitjacket fit her nicely.

Deirdre (thankfully) pulled through her operations, and I went to visit her a week after the accident. I apologized for leaving her on the side of the road, explained I thought she was fatally wounded and that I was still under attack. She graciously understood. Said the safety of her niece was the most important thing.

John was not so forgiving. He pulled me aside in the lobby of the hospital.

"You shouldn't have left her there."

I said, "John, you have no idea how badly I feel about that."

"I don't care how you feel. She could have died out there."

"You don't understand." I didn't know what else to say. Didn't know how much he knew.

John stared me down. Finally, he dropped his pants and mooned me.

On his ass was the mark of the Guardian.

I knew I had forgotten to check something when I caught up with Sayer at the Shelby farm.

John said he had just gotten the confirmation from the council on the Warrior and was about to make contact when the call came that Deirdre had been shot.

I asked him if he knew what "Mahoney money" meant (Ivy had mentioned "phony money" and I thought maybe she had been mistaken). He explained that his family was the wealthiest of the three clans, and it was determined that any funding needed for the cause would be set up in a trust for all three families to use as needed at the discretion of the council.

"Until next time," he said and walked back into his wife's room.

It was Friday afternoon when Chance walked into my office.

"Hey, gorgeous. You ready?" He came over and brushed his lips across my neck. Then he sat on my desk and pulled me to him, his blue eyes warm and inviting.

I stood, draped my arms around his neck, and kissed him thoroughly. It felt safe to be in his embrace. As much as I cared for Leo, Chance was the one who knew me best. We had a history that couldn't be shaken. And even though he could be a tad protective, he trusted my judgment and accepted me for who I was, flying imaginary squirrels and all.

Besides, if a man can forgive you for crashing his truck, he's worth a second look.

"What do you say we get some take-out and go to my place?" he asked.

"Only if it involves chocolate syrup," I said.

"Oh, that could be arranged."

I leaned across my desk to grab my bag when the phone rang.

"Don't answer it," Chance said.

I smiled. "Two minutes."

The voice on the other end of the line was gruff. "Stacy Justice?"

"Speaking."

"Stacy Justice the second, right?"

"Yes."

Chance tickled me and I laughed.

"I just thought you should know that I have the tapes."

"What tapes?" I asked, slapping Chance's hands away.

The man on the phone swore softly. "You haven't gone through his files yet, have you?"

"Whose files? What are you talking about?"

Chance looked at me, concerned. He raised his hand, questioningly. I shrugged.

"It wasn't an accident," the man said.

I sat down in my chair, that creepy-crawly feeling climbing up my spine. "Who is this?"

A pause. Then he repeated it. "It wasn't an accident. Your father was murdered."

Click.

~END~

Author's Note

While writers often take great liberties in fiction, much of what you have just read comes from hours of research. I thought fans of my work might be interested to know that there is indeed a Ballymote book and it resides within the halls of the Royal Irish Academy.

The first page is still missing.

You may be surprised to learn that Ogham was a written language and that in northern Europe today there are approximately five hundred known stone carvings engraved with this script.

This is what it looks like:

Translation:
Money is honored, without money nobody is loved

Now, what about the zombie powder, you ask? Well, that too is an actual poison derived from the puffer fish and has been used as Fiona described.

Sadly, the antidote is not bat poop.

This book takes place sometime between Imbolc and Ostara, the spring equinox. Ostara occurs around March 21, when the balance of light and dark is equal. It's a day when the world has one foot in the dead of winter and one aimed toward the birth of spring. Rituals vary on this day and may include chasing winter away via a banishing spell or spring "cleaning" with a sage smudge stick. Egg decorating is also popular this time of year. Eggs symbolize fertility and life—much like mother earth is awakening, preparing to accept new seeds into her belly.

Below are some recipes to wake up your body and soul from a long, harsh winter.

Salmon en Croute

In Celtic mythology, the salmon is a magical fish that grants the eater knowledge of all things.

Notes:

Nonstick spray may be substituted for melted butter.

Keep the phyllo covered with plastic wrap and a damp towel until ready to assemble; otherwise, it will dry out.

2 cloves garlic
1 7-oz. jar sun-dried tomatoes in olive oil
3 cups torn fresh basil leaves
salt and pepper to taste

1 package 9x14 phyllo dough, thawed
1 cup melted butter
10 4-oz. salmon fillets, skin removed
2 eggs, beaten with ¼ cup water

Preheat oven to 425 degrees. In a food processor, blend garlic, tomatoes with oil, basil, and salt and pepper. Set aside. Grease two large cookie sheets. Carefully lay five sheets of phyllo across each cookie sheet, overlapping and brushing each sheet with melted butter. Repeat. Divide salmon evenly between the cookie sheets and place vertically on top of phyllo, leaving a space between each fillet. Divide and spread basil mixture on top of each individual salmon fillet. Cover salmon with five sheets of phyllo, brushing each sheet with butter. Repeat. With a pizza cutter or knife, slice in between each fillet. Using egg wash, fold sides of phyllo together to form individual "packets." Bake for 15–20 minutes. Serves 10.

Lemon Zucchini Bake

Use lemon thyme to add a sweet citrus flavor to everything from poultry to vegetables. If you can't find it in your area, try chopped lemon balm, lemon verbena, or lemon basil.

¼ cup seasoned bread crumbs
¼ cup grated Parmesan cheese
2 teaspoons lemon thyme leaves
2 large zucchinis, thinly sliced
1 large Vidalia onion, thinly sliced
4 tablespoons melted butter

Preheat oven to 350 degrees. Mix bread crumbs, cheese, and thyme. In a round casserole dish, layer half of the zucchini and half of the onion slices. Baste with melted butter. Add half of the bread crumb mixture. Repeat layers and bake, covered, for 20 minutes. Serves 4–6.

Body Scrub

Sugar scrubs are a great way to slough off stress and dead skin. For unique scents, try layering dried herbs like lavender (revitalizing) or peppermint (energizing) with a cup of white sugar and let stand for two weeks before use, shaking periodically. Then blend with a tablespoon of light oil such as sunflower seed. Slough away dead skin in the shower or tub.

Also by Barbra Annino

Opal Fire: Stacy Justice Book One
Tiger's Eye: Stacy Justice Book Three
Gnome Wars: A Short Story
Doppelganger: A Novella
Every Witch Way but Wicked: An Anthology (includes a Stacy Justice story)

About the Author

Photo by George Annino, 2011

Barbra Annino is a native of Chicago, a book junkie, and a Springsteen addict. She's worked as a bartender and humor columnist, and currently lives in picturesque Galena, Illinois, where she ran a bed-and-breakfast for five years. She now writes fiction full-time—when she's not walking her three Great Danes.

Made in the USA
Charleston, SC
14 April 2013